# WAITING FOR EDEN

Center Point
Large Print

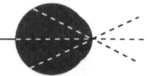

**This Large Print Book carries the
Seal of Approval of N.A.V.H.**

# WAITING FOR EDEN

Elliot Ackerman

CENTER POINT LARGE PRINT
THORNDIKE, MAINE

This Center Point Large Print edition
is published in the year 2018 by arrangement with
Alfred A. Knopf, an imprint of
The Knopf Doubleday Publishing Group,
a division of Penguin Random House, LLC.

The text of this Large Print edition is unabridged.
In other aspects, this book may vary
from the original edition.
Printed in the United States of America
on permanent paper.
Set in 16-point Times New Roman type.

ISBN: 978-1-68324-978-8

Library of Congress Cataloging-in-Publication Data

Names: Ackerman, Elliot, author.
Title: Waiting for Eden / Elliot Ackerman.
Description: Center Point Large Print edition. | Thorndike, Maine :
    Center Point Large Print, 2018.
Identifiers: LCCN 2018036580 | ISBN 9781683249788
    (hardcover : alk. paper)
Subjects: LCSH: Large type books.
Classification: LCC PS3601.C5456 W35 2018b | DDC 813/.6—dc23
LC record available at https://lccn.loc.gov/2018036580

For My Mother

# WAITING FOR EDEN

I want you to understand Mary and what she did. But I don't know if you will. You've got to wonder if in the end you'd make the same choice, circumstances being similar, or even the same, God help you. Back when I first met her and Eden times were better. They were trying to start a family then. And months later, on that night in the Hamrin Valley, I was sitting next to Eden and luckier than him when our Humvee hit a pressure plate, killing me and everybody else, him barely surviving.

Ever since then I've been around too, just on that other side, seeing all there is, and waiting.

Three years have gone by and my friend's spent every day of it laid out in that burn center in San Antonio. I could give you the catalogue of his injuries, but I won't. Not because I don't think you could stomach it, but because I don't think it'd really tell you much about what type of a way he's in. So I'll tell you this: he used to weigh 220 pounds, and some mornings, when we'd work out together, he'd press well over 150 above his head, sweat pouring from beneath his black hair. Before we deployed, he and I both went to SERE school, that's the one up in Maine where they teach you what to do in case

9

you become a prisoner. For a couple of weeks the instructors starved us and roughed us up pretty bad. Then the course ended and those same instructors had a graduation party with us. That night at the party, I watched him pound five pints of Guinness in almost as many minutes. He held it all down, too. But I'll also tell you that if you ever went to his house for dinner he wouldn't serve Guinness, he'd likely do all the cooking and serve you a bottle of wine he'd chosen specially for your visit. He could tell you all about the wine: the viticulture considerations in the soil of the vineyard, the seasonal high and low temperatures of the year it was bottled, and when you were done with that and the main course, he'd serve chocolate with hot pepper or sea salt, or some other fancy thing mixed in. He said that stuff brought out the flavor. I still don't know if that's true, but I liked that he said it. I'll tell you that every guy in the platoon had a nickname. One pervy guy was called Hand Job because he had all sorts of weird porn on his computer. And another guy, a kind of dumb guy, was called Wedge because a wedge is the world's simplest tool. But Eden's nickname was BASE Jump. One time during a hurricane party at the barracks he'd gotten drunk and with a poncho spread over his head he leaped from the third deck. When the wind carried him a bit and he landed on both feet, the name was his. That's how he treated the whole world, too, like it was a series of cliffs that existed for no other reason than for him to jump off. At least before the pressure plate. But now I don't know what to call him. The 70 pounds that's left of him in the bed—he's had a lot of infections, and they've cut all of him off up to the torso—isn't BASE Jump and it isn't the name he was born with. I don't think anyone really knows what to call him, except for Mary. She calls him her husband.

Mary was pregnant the day he touched down at the air base in San Antonio and she's been there every day since. After the pressure plate, they almost didn't fly him out of Balad. The docs there were sure he was about to go, and they were doubly sure the trip would kill him. Still they were obligated to at least try and get him home.

On the C-17 back two nurses stayed within arm's length of him the whole ride. Also on the flight was a kid from the 82nd Airborne, a private first class. The kid had been shot in the ass. Had the bullet gone half an inch higher, it would've nicked off some of his spine, instead it nicked off some of his lower intestine, a bit of good luck. Another bit of good luck for the kid was Eden. My friend's emergency flight to San Antonio got the kid a direct flight to his hometown, otherwise he would've been sent back on the biweekly rotator through Bethesda.

The kid spent the whole flight laid out on a gurney just across from Eden's. He was strapped down on his stomach, a big and humiliating piece of gauze stuck into his wound. My friend was burnt up so bad that the kid couldn't tell which way they'd strapped him to his gurney, on his front or on his back.

The kid was in pain but doing all right. He was on a solid morphine drip. What bothered him more than his wounds were the pair of nurses who talked too loud and the bright lights in the cabin. The lights were kept bright so open wounds could be seen clearly by the nurses. Still the lights kept the kid awake. My friend kept the kid awake too, trying to sleep next to someone as burnt up as him was like trying to sleep next to a box of poisonous snakes.

But knowing what type of a way Eden was in made the kid feel a bit better about the type of a way he was in. All along the docs had told the kid he wasn't too bad off. They'd even said once he got sewed up and put back together he'd be in no worse shape than someone who'd had a real bad hernia. The kid didn't buy that line, but on the plane, headed home and looking at my friend, he did start to feel a bit better.

During the flight, a male nurse came to check on the kid every couple of hours. The nurse made sure he was comfortable and looked over his bandages and vitals. About halfway home, the C-17 landed at Ramstein Air Base to refuel. That's when the male nurse, the one who'd been looking after the kid, got off the plane. Once they got back in the air a different nurse, a young one who was also watching Eden, came by to check on the kid.

"You're looking all right," she said.

"You know it," replied the kid, and he gave her a flirty smile. She had good dark skin and her black hair was pulled tightly into a bun.

"Your ass is seeping a bit," said the young nurse. "Get some sleep. I'll change you before we land." She covered him with a blanket.

The kid didn't say anything. He pushed the button on his clicker for another shot from his morphine drip. He didn't want to look at her anymore so he turned his head back to the bulkhead, trying to sleep.

Then the young nurse went to check on Eden. When she stood over him, he was shuddering on his gurney. She read his temperature. It was high, dangerously so. His skin, already see-through with burns, didn't sweat, it couldn't. Instead it shone, the fever trapped inside. The second, older nurse came over. As she did, his body seized and then did a sort of *whip-crack,* struggling for breath even as he gasped. Without speaking, the older nurse ran to the refrigerator at the front of the plane. That's where they kept the blood.

The two nurses worked together searching for a place to transfuse the blood into my friend. Their movements were mechanical and silent. Their hands raced unfamiliarly over his body, not recognizing the places where they could usually find enough vein for a needle. Soon the young nurse found a soft patch of skin on his side.

She flicked the skin with her finger. Slowly it turned red as a sunburn. Then, beneath the red, she found a dark and lurking vein. She angled the needle to the vein and lanced it in, hooking up the tubing. Blood barely trickled through. It met great resistance and didn't flow as it should. Instead it percolated like the last drips of coffee from a machine. His body was shutting down, rejecting what was offered it. Still the nurses kept up their work, massaging the bag of blood, fighting off the collapse of his veins as if the transfused red and white cells were a squad of workmen desperately jointing the rafters of a house ready to fall in on itself. Then slowly the bag began to empty into his body. And through hydraulics my friend stayed alive.

Over Eden, the two nurses took up a vigil. The older nurse stood at the head of his bed. She massaged the bag of blood. The younger nurse stood at his side. She kept the thick needle in place, pressing it to his skin. Inside him, the needle's beveled point held to the single and narrow vein like a climber with too few fingers on a ledge.

For three hours, the nurses hardly spoke.

Then the C-17's engine ground against the air, slowing. Both nurses yawned, their ears popping in the descent. Eden groaned, feeling the pain in his ears, despite every other thing he could've felt. The kid lay across from them, facing the bulkhead, soundless and peacefully unaware of the quiet struggle occurring next to him.

The C-17 banked as they flew their final approach. The two nurses watched as Eden's temperature crept safely downward, the fresh blood saving him. His fever dropped, his progress mirroring the flight's descent. When the C-17 touched down, its tires smoking the runway, the young nurse recorded his final temperature: a low-grade fever, exactly as it'd been on takeoff sixteen hours before.

They taxied down the runway, the flightless wings of the C-17 sagging heavily toward the ground. The young nurse and the old nurse stood on either side of my friend's gurney, poised like a couple of bobsledders, ready to get him off the C-17 and on his way to the burn center. An unspoken satisfaction passed between the two nurses. This flight had been historic in a way. My friend was, they'd been told, the most wounded man from both the wars. As advanced as medicine had become, that likely made him the most wounded man in the history of war, and they'd just kept him alive from one side of the world to the other.

Over the C-17's engine there was a distinct thumping in the air. The young nurse leaned into one of the plane's portholes. A white helicopter with a red cross idled on the tarmac. All of this for just one patient, she thought. Her mind wandered and she recalled something she'd read or heard once, in a place she couldn't quite remember, about how the suffering of the world is in the suffering of the individual and that in the individual is all the world, or something like that. Even though she couldn't remember the whole idea, she liked what it said about her and her work, and as the C-17 taxied toward the helicopter, she mulled over these thoughts and what it meant that they'd saved Eden.

Red and green taillights and runway lights pulsed in the early morning fog. The back ramp of the C-17 gaped open. The nurses ran my friend down the ramp. They passed his gurney over to a handful of paramedics, who took it with all the frenzy of a pit crew. Then the older nurse ran back into the C-17. She'd forgotten to give the paramedics his chart. She returned down the ramp and scrambled onto the tarmac, clasping the chart to her chest as its papers threatened to blow away in the downwash of the many engines. Already the white helicopter pitched and whined, beginning to take off. She ran toward it. Lucky for her, one of the paramedics looked up at that moment. He saw her coming and she managed to hand him the chart. The older nurse then walked back over to the C-17. On its ramp sat the young nurse. She untied her black hair, ran her fingers through it, and then with several twists of her wrist pulled it once again into a bun. The two sat together, looking off.

The young nurse stared down the runway, in the direction the white helicopter had left, toward the distant lights of San Antonio. "Who's meeting him at the hospital?" she asked the old nurse.

"A burn triage team."

"That's not what I meant," said the young nurse.

The old nurse looked back at her. "I don't know. I didn't want to ask."

The two stood and walked back up the ramp.

In the C-17, the kid still lay on his side, facing the bulkhead. The young nurse rested her palm on his shoulder. He didn't move. Quickly she touched his forehead with the back of her hand. It was cold. She planted her index and middle fingers on his neck. Nothing. She put her cheek inches from his mouth. She felt no breath and his face was the same as in sleep.

The old nurse pulled the blanket away.

Around the kid's legs and hips the flesh was tight and swollen. The old nurse put her hands on him there. He was still warm and there was a fullness that sloshed like a hot water bottle.

Footsteps came up the C-17's ramp, a lone paramedic. Parked behind him was a regular ambulance.

"Hell of a job, you two," he said. Then he pulled a Motorola off his belt and wagged it at them. "They're five minutes out and he's still stable. You wanna get your other guy loaded up?"

The old nurse leaned heavily against the kid's gurney. She reached up, handing over his chart. "Bled into himself," she said. "We missed it."

The paramedic glanced down at the kid. "Looks like he went quick."

Then the three of them rolled his gurney out to the parked ambulance, taking their time with it.

n the papers and on cable news they counted the dead from the two wars separately, giving each a running number. For ten hours the kid made Iraq's number 816, then another kid in Ramadi by way of Spokane made it 817. Splitting the numbers kept each figure manageable, but on the night Eden came in Mary began to add the numbers. To her, the kid's number was 1,314. At first she thought her husband's number would fall somewhere around there. At first she always knew the latest number plus one, thinking that number would become forever familiar to her. But Eden held on. After a while she began to wonder about very far-off sums, ones that had never seemed possible before.

Slowly she changed her mind about what his number might be. But she always knew he'd have a number. That wouldn't change, no matter how long he held on. For in the end it would always be the war that killed him. And so the war could never be over, the final number could never be counted as long as my friend waited in that hospital bed. At times she felt almost special knowing this, as though her husband held some great power of ending. But this wasn't true. He wasn't special at all. There were many others who the war was just waiting to kill and then count.

For three years Mary counted, never once leaving him. Family came and went, both his and hers. But she was the only one who stayed. A few months after he got there, she gave birth two floors down in the same hospital. Minutes after the birth, the nurses wheeled her and her new daughter up into his room. They put their gurney next to his. The room was quiet. The baby was very well behaved: when she looked at Eden, she stopped crying.

Her baby daughter, nicknamed Andy, grew all through that first year. Soon she looked more like a girl than a baby, and her hair came in and it was fiery and red. In both his family and hers there were many remarks that no one had ever had hair like Andy's. One of the doctors remarked that emotional trauma to the mother often led to certain recessive genes becoming dominant.

In the months after Andy was born, Eden's brother and sister, all the family he had left, decided he should be let go. They were both much older and with children of their own. When they spoke to Mary about this they told her of Eden's aunt, who'd raised all of them, and how when she'd become sick they'd done everything to extend her life and all it had amounted to was the pain of a slow death. They said all this to Mary many different times and in many different ways, always asking her to let go of Eden. Always she said no. After they asked for the last time, they went home, had a memorial service for their brother and stopped visiting the burn center in San Antonio. They also stopped visiting the redheaded girl.

Mary would never leave him. Soon Eden became like an appendage to her, one she spoke for. Grafts, hydrogel treatments, cleanings, all decided by her. His body became her own, and she anchored to it. Even as she refused to leave, she wanted him to die. She just had to look at her daughter, Andy, to feel that want. The girl's first steps were taken down the linoleum hallways of the burn center. After that first year, guilt for her daughter overcame guilt for her husband. A few nights after those first steps, she called her mother and asked if Andy could stay back east with her. They both agreed the girl would visit the hospital every few months, seeing her mother only, being spared visits with Eden, and that this new arrangement would be just for a little while. But neither would say until when.

Then, on the third Christmas, Mary decided to go home and spend the holiday with her daughter and mother. There was no specific reason, except that she'd come to feel he might never die and that what little remained of him might live even longer than she. The doctors encouraged her, of course. They told her that on a subconscious and emotional level her happiness would help him find some peace. She thought maybe that was true. They also told her that he wouldn't even know she was gone. This she couldn't believe. If it were true, it meant all the time she'd spent at the hospital didn't matter.

The whole week before her trip, she camped out on the sofa in Eden's room. But it was only the day of her flight that she told him she was leaving.

"I'll celebrate with you when I come back," she said.

The motor on his breathing pump kicked into gear.

She climbed up on his bed and leaned in, not touching his burns but so close that her smell would linger around him. Before, when they would be in bed together, she'd often wake when he'd bury his face deep into the nape of her neck, covering himself in her dark hair to what she worried was the point of suffocation. One of the first things he ever told her was that he liked her perfume, but she never wore any. Her smell was of soap and water.

"I'll get some pictures of Andy opening the dollhouse," she told him.

My friend stared across the room, the blue in his gaze running to gray, walleyed and just gone. Then he blinked a couple of times.

Between the blinks, she thought he looked at

her real quick. She stared at him but his eyes were now fixed across the room. She decided that was enough. It was enough of a sign that he understood, she thought.

She'd long been warned by the doctors about too much skin-on-skin contact with him, especially on the face, so she kissed the pillow next to his cheek.

She left that afternoon. In the morning it'd be Christmas, and over the next three days he'd come awake.

I t's not pleasant to say or to think on, but up until that Christmas the parts of Eden his wife and doctors obsessed over weren't much. He's my friend so I can say this, and in a quiet moment the doctors would tell you the same. They'd explain how he was brain damaged: thirty percent reduction in frontal lobe activity, fifty percent reduction in parietal lobe activity, contusions throughout. That's how it was. Even if you forgot about the burns, the blast had cleaved his helmet right in two. And the little of him that was still there, well, it was difficult to call that him. He had a mind all right, but it'd become like a twice-cut jigsaw, pieces in the pieces.

He'd forgotten a lot. Or maybe the old things just meant less. For instance, he no longer remembered the name of the valley where it all happened, the Hamrin, but he knew the smell of burnt pine and the painful way the dry mountain air used to crack bloody fissures into his lips and the inside of his nose. He didn't remember that he'd been a corporal in 1st Battalion, 6th Marines, but he did remember what it felt like to be far from home, wanting to kill but afraid of death. He remembered he'd had friends who'd felt the same.

I know he remembered me.

As Mary told Eden about her Christmas plans, he listened but didn't really hear her. He was busy staring across the room. The linoleum floor shone perfectly except for in the far corner, where a small panel was missing. Here, in the grouting, hair and oily dust-scum collected. But he wasn't looking at the filth. He was looking at a cockroach that stood in it. That entire week while Mary camped out on Eden's sofa, this cockroach had been roaming the room just staring at him.

Eden didn't know the name for a cockroach anymore, but he knew that its hard-backed shell and thorny legs could run a number on him. He didn't know his wife's name either, but she had just kissed his pillow and he knew the smoothness of her dark hair and her soap-and-water smell. All week she'd been by his bed, and he'd felt the sadness of her slow and heavy movements, but he'd been distracted too. He kept thinking, Look at that bug, fuck man. Sitting there across the room, it was trouble. The cockroach had crept close a couple of times. It'd already gotten up on the foot of his bed once. My friend's legs had cramped with fear then, even though he didn't have legs. He'd tried to stare down the cockroach with a concentration that bordered on telekinesis. He'd seen its tentacles shoot straight up, like the cockroach knew how powerful Eden's mind was and that the dumb bug would have to scheme up a better way to sneak onto the bed.

His first night alone was Christmas Eve, that's when she left. Not long after the sun went down someone, he didn't know who, came in and shut off the lights. Eden's blank eyes patrolled the room. He couldn't see, but he could smell that cockroach, crawling out there. To him, its scent was puke and fear, swirling invisibly around his bed. Even though he strained to stay one step ahead of the bug, eventually he drifted to sleep. But in his dreams, he looked for that fucker.

My friend was exhausted. He never knew if and when he slept.

Then, in what seemed like the middle of the night, he heard a noise from the window ledge behind him. It came quickly, intoning thunder. He knew what it was: a thousand of those cockroaches, an entire brigade of thorny feet clopping behind him. He could feel the vibrations of their march. They rattled his sheets against his skin. Listening to the endless iterations, he began to sweat, the wet salt bubbling up through his few unmelted pores, then soaking back into his wounds. The sting of it. He could now feel every exposure of his body and in these places he felt his pulse and heartbeat. They pounded together, wild as native drums.

Then it all stopped.

He ground his teeth in the new silence. They

were coming for him, he was certain. He sniffed the air. Their smell was gone. He didn't know why, but this made him more afraid. With his blitzed eyes, he strained to glimpse just one of them. He wanted that least bit of dignity, which was to see them coming before they ran up his bed and into his wounds and stumps, pouring down his throat. He kept sweating. He couldn't stop and it burned many parts of him. Other parts it didn't. He didn't feel anything there, and this reminded him that those other parts were dead. Still he waited. If he could've spoken, he would've said: "C'mon, you fuckers! Come get some!" He would've been scared shitless as he said it, but he would've.

He did nothing and the room remained quiet.

It was quiet for a long time.

Just when he thought he'd imagined the entire cockroach army, he heard them again, thousands of their invisible legs banging behind his bed, near the window ledge, a miniature phalanx of ancient soldiers striking swords on shields, all in unison, all in the cadence of advance. He knew they'd crawl over him before he could even get a look and he did the only thing he could: he waited.

When the sun rose that's what he was still doing.

Mary went home. The next morning she woke up on the floor of her old room, now her daughter's room. It was very early on Christmas. She'd gotten in the night before and after putting Andy to bed she couldn't bring herself to leave the room so she slept there, wrapped in a comforter. She'd always been a side sleeper, but the carpet was thin and the hard floorboards put an ache in her hip, which woke her. She propped herself up on her elbows, bringing her face level with the edge of her old bed. The girl slept deeply, and her red hair tumbled off the side of the bed toward the carpet.

The room was dark, becoming dim. Mary crawled to the window and stood, the comforter falling from her shoulders like a lost skin. She twisted the wand on the blinds to close the slats. Andy stirred at the little bit of noise. With the slats shut, it was very dark again. Mary crept across the room avoiding the places where she knew the floorboards creaked. She left the door open a crack. The house was quiet except for the noise of faraway birds growing slowly louder.

Everyone would sleep for another hour, she thought. Downstairs she put her coat over her sweats and stepped into the narrow backyard of the row house. Two troughs of soil flanked the yard. In the night there'd been a dusting of wet snow. It layered the black plastic sheets that protected the frozen and fallow rows. The spring before Mary's mother had taken pictures of Andy seeding the rows. Months later her mother took more pictures of the girl, picking what she'd grown. She'd sent the photos to Mary and each one was very bright: the green lattices of stalked crops, and the reds and yellows of tomatoes and squash resting heavily in the dirt. Between the troughs were a stone side table and wicker chair. In the warm weather this is where her mother read.

Mary stepped around the side of the house. Here the trash cans were kept in a narrow passageway that led to the street. The trash cans were now all plastic. When she'd last visited they'd been aluminum. There was a small brick step there. She dusted the new snow from it and sat. From her pocket, she pulled out a pack of cigarettes and some wooden matches. The morning was very still. Her match struck loudly. The smoke she exhaled billowed into the cold air, tumbling into clouds.

Her mother didn't know that she'd started smoking again, but her mother never knew that she had smoked. It was one of the first things she'd learned to hide, and now it seemed easier to keep hiding it in the old way. When she finished her first cigarette, she stood and reached under the clapboards at the bottom of the house. She felt around, palming frozen soil and paint chips. Then, from beneath a familiar trestle, she pulled up an old coffee can half filled with cigarette butts. She opened its lid. It'd been there a long time and she thought it would stink, but in the cold it didn't. She finished her cigarette, dipped its cherry into the snow and tossed the wet butt in the can. Then she smoked a second. She didn't know when she'd have a chance for another.

She heard her mother in the house and before her second cigarette was finished she snubbed out its cherry in the can. Then she shut the lid and reached back up under the clapboards, hiding the can. She took a stick of gum from her coat pocket and walked around to the front porch. There was a spigot here and she washed her hands in its cold water. She then grabbed the newspaper off the front steps and walked back inside.

The house opened into the den. There her mother sat at a wooden table, wrapping the last few gifts for Andy. Mary hung her coat by the door and sat the newspaper on the table. Her mother finished with the gifts and began to read it. Her mouth moved around each word, drawing wrinkles into the softness of her skin like a separate and disappearing text, and her manicured hands pulled against her thinning hair, which was a mix of black and gray like smoke from burning plastic.

Mary crossed the den and walked into the connecting kitchen. She began to cook breakfast. She added eggs, milk and oil to an expired box of pancake mix. She whisked the ingredients together. There was a dish of cut strawberries in the refrigerator. She didn't ask what they might be for, but instead she added them to the batter. Then she laid slabs of bacon on a paper towel.

The pilot light on the burner clicked stubbornly, refusing to catch a flame. She looked at her mother, who was still reading, not watching her, so she took the matches from the pocket of her sweats and lit the stove. She greased the skillet and poured out the first of the batter. It spit in the heat, small bits landing on the skillet's walls, burning quickly. She turned down the flame. Slowly, the batter fattened as it warmed, its edges bubbling to porousness.

The noise of cooking was very loud now. The sun was up too.

Mary reached into the cupboard and brought down plastic dishes. All the cups and plates were mismatched. She couldn't find a set of three. She put them away and climbed on top of the counter. From her knees she could reach the high cabinets and her mother's china. She gently sat down three plates, trimmed in gold. She brought down three crystal goblets, too, and from a far drawer laid out some unpolished silver. The top plate was very dusty, so were the goblets. She wiped her hands against her sweatpants and cleaned everything by the sink, then she set the table in the den.

As Mary did this, she heard the skillet sizzle on the stove, spitting again. Her mother had forked the bacon onto it, having come into the kitchen to take over the cooking. Mary glanced at her mother, who now ran the edge of the fork under the dark brown rims of the pancakes.

"Not like that," Mary said. "Do it with a spatula."

Her mother looked at her like she was a child and, disregarding her protest, flipped over the first pancake with the fork. It landed perfectly. She spoke to her daughter but watched the skillet: "We'll be late if you don't get Andy up."

"I'd rather let her sleep."

"You know, I don't force her come to church with me, she likes it."

Mary climbed the stairs toward her daughter's room. Before she could get to the door, Andy reached up and opened it. She stood, leaning against the jamb, her hand still on the knob, upset in the way children often are in the mornings, frightened by new days. Her face was wet and a little swollen, and Mary petted away the wetness. Andy rubbed her eye with a little fist and then reached up with both arms. Mary scooped the girl onto her hip. Andy had turned three a few months before, but was very slender and long limbed. Mary worried she was thin in ways she couldn't afford, though Mary's mother didn't have this worry and said the girl was just plain skinny.

Andy rested her head on Mary's shoulder. The girl's red hair mixed with her mother's black hair. From the top of the stairs, the house smelled of pancakes and bacon. At first the girl turned away, not wanting to eat breakfast, but when she heard her grandmother moving in the kitchen, she struggled from Mary's arms. Andy held on to the banister as she took the stairs slowly, one at a time, making sure not to trip on the hem of her nightgown. Her grandmother served them both pancakes and bacon on the mismatched plastic dishes, and the two gathered around the Christmas tree.

Mary said nothing, but went to the wooden table she'd set with the china and gathered it back up into the high cabinet while her mother and daughter ate on the other side of the small row house.

"If you aren't going to have breakfast," her mother called out, "help us get started with the presents."

"In a second. I want to check in with the hospital," Mary said. At first she moved through the house, slow and deliberate, searching for her phone in the obvious places: her purse, her suitcase, the pockets of her coat, but it was in none of those. Then she checked her daughter's room, and the crumpled comforter on the floor. She came back downstairs, walking and rewalking where she'd come in the night before.

Grandmother and granddaughter finished their breakfasts. They sat by the tree waiting and Andy began to ask about her presents. Her grandmother told her to wait just a little more.

Mary used the kitchen phone to call herself. It went to voicemail. She did this again and again, moving through the house in a panic, telling her mother and daughter to be quiet as she listened for her phone ringing or vibrating. While Mary searched, her mother let Andy open a few of the gifts. When Mary saw this, she stopped looking for a moment, not wanting to miss the time with her daughter. She sat on the floor and watched Andy tear through the wrapping paper. She also looked up at the Christmas tree, which towered above them. Lights circled it as it peaked against the ceiling. Tucked into its branches were decades of ornaments passed down through the family. There was an ivory bulb dusted with gold, a reminder of Mary's father. Unlit among the electric lights were three silver candleholders, survivors of a much larger set that had been her great-grandmother's.

Mary ran her eyes over the tree, searching for one decoration in particular. It was a picture of her and Eden from before. It hung in a silver snowflake frame, and she couldn't find it. She wondered where on the tree it was hidden, or if her mother had made the decision to leave it off the tree this year, or maybe if her mother had thrown it out, not wanting to look at it, ever.

Once Andy finished opening her presents, her grandmother said it was time for everyone to get ready for church. The girl headed up to her room with a new stuffed toy in a headlock.

"I still don't like that you take her," said Mary.

"I wish you'd come," replied her mother.

Mary looked away. "The only contact I gave the hospital was my cell."

Her mother didn't say anything, but walked to the kitchen phone. She dialed a number written on a green Post-it and handed the receiver to Mary. After several transfers the line found its way to the shift nurse who was on call at the burn center. Mary explained about the lost phone and the shift nurse told her that Eden was fine and his condition stable. The shift nurse took down the number to the kitchen phone and said she'd call if anything happened.

"Now go change," her mother insisted.

Mary did as she was told and went upstairs to get ready for church. As she dressed she felt a bitter form of certainty. She knew her mother had thrown out the silver snowflake decoration a long time ago.

When Mary called to check up on her husband, the shift nurse had been reading one of those celebrity magazines, and after they spoke she went right back to it, licking her fingertips so they gripped the cheap waxy paper, her mind idling.

Eden and I used to read those magazines when we were deployed, waiting for a flight or a convoy, just trying to kill time. Whenever you're stuck somewhere with time to kill you can always find one of those magazines. I've often wondered if the people in their pages read them too. They're probably too busy. Now both he and I are killing a fuckload of time and neither of us has even so much as a single magazine.

That morning the shift nurse had yet to look in on Eden. She kept tabs on his vitals from the monitors at her desk, and hoped to finish her stint with him from there. Looking at him wasn't something she'd planned on doing. She was new to San Antonio, just months out of nursing school, and burns weren't her specialty, pediatrics were. She didn't want to see what she'd heard he was. Still, sitting at the burn center's main desk, alone, and on Christmas morning, she wondered

about him. Even though he powered the relentless pounding of vital signs that surrounded her desk, she didn't know if you could call what was in that room a person. Not alive, not dead, what it was didn't have a name.

She'd heard the stories about when they'd brought him in. The rush to the roof, his helicopter landing, and how close to death he'd always been. Between shifts, the older docs and nurses spoke quietly about the guy up on the fourth floor burned so bad it was a miracle he'd survived. They always talked about him quickly, in murmurs over their coffee or standing close to each other in an elevator. What they'd say was always the same: worst wounded guy in both wars, don't know if I'd want to live like that, and just a matter of time. They all said that one: a matter of time. And Jesus Christ if it wasn't true. For my friend it was a matter of days, weeks, months, years, lying there, not being allowed to just die.

The shift nurse wondered how long he might live. Maybe someday he'd leave the hospital and go home. They all wanted that, but it'd never happen. And if it wouldn't, she thought he should at least get to die, but not getting to do that either, and for so long, well, that was enough to keep her from wanting to go into his room. She'd told herself that she'd just sit at her desk and watch the monitors. That was enough. She'd do that.

Then it'd be over. She'd go back to pediatrics and, she hoped, never draw a shift on the fourth floor again, especially not over Christmas.

Now, I may be making out this particular nurse to sound cold, but she wasn't. She was just too young and too tired to be dealing with the seventy pounds laid out down the hall from her.

On her desk was one of those little Christmas trees, like the one Snoopy used to put on his doghouse, all done up with lights, each bulb fat as a grape and each branch tangled with tinsel. After a while she felt all tight in her chest looking at it, knowing she was spending her Christmas with him, and his with her, and that this might be his last Christmas and with all that winding up inside her, she did the only thing she could do: she unplugged that Snoopy tree and took it down to his room.

Inside the room, the shades were drawn. Some light snuck out along the seams, glowing a bit, but mostly just graying the room. As the shift nurse came in, she didn't look at him, I mean not right at him. She looked around him. A set of monitors, same as those by her desk, sat next to him. Those machines and others surrounded his bed like a drum set, their tubes and cords running into his body as though he were the battery that powered them.

The squeak of her shoes against the floor's linoleum and the pump that breathed for him

were the only sounds in the room. She walked to the window and opened the blinds. A swell of light broke over Eden's bed. With the light came color, and she could see him now in a way she couldn't before. The white of his linens, the little pink stains where pieces of him had stuck against them, the great hollows of his wounds, dark and asking to be stared into. She found colors there she'd never known in a person before, but they were inside him and, by that measure, inside her. The browns, the greens, and the subcutaneous yellows of deep scars coiled like knotted yarn against his skin and deeper, and she saw his eyes and they blinked at her, unprotected by lashes, and she could see where they were rheumy without rest and soapy with pain, and how they teared against his pillow, always.

She shut the blinds.

A heater blew against her hands. It was mounted inside a vented ledge beneath the window. She set the Snoopy tree on the ledge and searched for an outlet. She found one behind his bed and plugged in the tree next to a cellphone that had been left there. Now the tree's lights filled the room with the twinkling of Crayola-pure colors: red, blue, yellow, green. She looked at him and his eyes followed her as she made for the door. Then, as she passed by the foot of his bed, she wanted to touch him. Her heart beat fast, its rhythm like fingertips thrumming anxiously against a table. She felt a little sweat ease down the arch of her back, in that place where her skin was softest and faintly layered with hair.

Now she came to the side of his bed.

His eyes looked away from her, toward the tree, and she could see the lights reflecting off their sheen. She moved her hand over him, and put the pad of her middle finger on one of the gauzy bandages that covered his side. Then she ran her finger up to the edge of the bandage and looked at his eyes again, and seeing that they saw nothing, her finger leapt from the bandage's edge onto the bare skin of his chest. It was burnt and smoked, bloodless, but not lifeless. This surprised her. The little piece of flesh she touched had more struggle in it than her whole body. Beneath her finger was survival, it was what a body could and would be when battered just to the edge. It was man suffering into the anlage of whatever came next, the amphibian crawling onto land, the first primate standing upright. It was that grotesque and purest form of adaptation: life.

She took her hand away.

Still he didn't look at her. He watched the Snoopy tree and the lights. She walked quickly out the door and back to her desk, behind the monitors. She wanted to read her magazine but couldn't.

She sat.

Eventually she managed to thumb through the first few pages, but only after she'd gone to the bathroom and washed her hand.

Before the shift nurse came in with the tree, Eden had been getting ready for a fight. The way he'd counted it, he'd seen that last cockroach, the one in the corner, almost a day ago. But even if that was the only one he'd seen, he'd heard thousands of them coming through the walls, popping blisters in the paint, like your head in a bowl of Rice Krispies with the volume turned up, louder than hell. The way they'd been going at it back there, he could almost see them row on row, their thorny legs and hard little rust-backs in close-order drill formation, all ready to swallow him down.

When the phone rang out in the hall and he heard the shift nurse talking to Mary, he thought the last he'd hear of his wife was her being told the lie that he was fine. This knot of thoughts is what was going through my friend's head when the shift nurse came in with the Snoopy tree, and goddamn if he didn't think she'd saved his life and scared off the cockroaches.

Eden was just about blind, so he didn't really see the shift nurse come in, what he saw was a flash of white move toward him, and he also saw the lights of the tree. They blinked like a neon sign through the window of a bad hotel room and

44

he could feel them on his face. But thank God for the lights, they'd keep the cockroaches away, he hoped. He also felt it when the nurse touched him, and he became embarrassed as he got a big raging phantom of a nonexistent hard-on, tickling all the way up to his burnt-out smear of a belly button. And he lay there wondering why that ability had come back only once everything was gone and he thought of the nurse's soap-and-water smell. He wheezed it through his nose, soap and water, soap and water. It took him back to his wife, and before that to his own skin in the shower and the way his fingers would squeak against its wetness, and the smell of his aunt's wrists when she'd pick him up when he was a boy. Soon he'd breathed in so much of that smell that he'd pulled it all out of the room, and the pump in the corner by his bed had processed all the soap and water there could be.

What came next was different and stronger.

He smelled the Snoopy tree in the corner, the pine sap and dry needles ready to fall to the floor. But this wasn't a Christmas smell for him, not anymore. No way it could be. This was the smell of granite slopes in low fog, mean tight roads, and well-fed sheikhs and self-appointed emirs with wax in their night-dark mustaches and their young men in the mountains, waiting for him. On the day he burned, this is what we both smelled in the truck mixing with diesel, our hair and bodies. Death smelled like a Snoopy tree.

He started breathing the pine in hard, trying to suck it all out of the room. He wanted a different smell. The pump worked in the corner and he along with it. He could feel his heart champing hard in his chest as he breathed out the pine smell, and then it was all gone and he waited for what would come next. He shut his eyes and on the backs of his lids he could still see the colors of the Christmas lights, each one exploding in planets of red, blue, yellow, green. His heart slowed and so did his breathing and then he opened his eyes and everything went to shit.

Standing right where he'd felt his phantom hard-on was the cockroach, staring at him, the lights flashing against his hard back: rusty red, rusty blue, rusty yellow, rusty green. Eden's heart started to eat a hole out of his chest. Then the cockroach's tentacles waggled in the air, and the fucker took one of his thorny legs and set it on the bottom of my friend's bandages, just taunting him, letting him know that he could climb anywhere he damn well wanted. Eden opened his eyes so wide and hard that tears ran down to his neck, the salt burning in the open parts of him. He tried to stare the cockroach off his bed as he'd done before.

It didn't work.

The cockroach stood there, looking at him. He was all black eyes beneath bowed tentacles.

Eden bucked his body against the bed.

46

Still the cockroach didn't move.

The pine smell left the room. The puke and fear smell of a thousand cockroaches replaced it, filling Eden's nostrils. Then, behind him, the vibrating sound of their thousand feet exploded. They were coming for him, he knew it; he gnashed his teeth, and just before he howled, he felt the great muscle of his heart tear in two.

The shift nurse was eating lunch at her desk, that's when she heard it, not his howl, but the monitors go off like an airplane losing altitude. Loud beeps and flashing screens, the great ascents and descents of his vital signs graphed out like the prospects of some collapsing enterprise. She pushed the emergency button at her desk. It was patched in to the senior nurse on call.

Then she ran into his room.

The monitors around his bed were going off too. He ground his teeth against the noise. He thrashed, bucking hard. She collapsed on his body, holding on, trying to keep the tubes and wires in him, and him in the bed. His strength surprised her. It was as though the ghosts of his limbs tossed and kicked at his torso while all three degrees of his burns rose up from his skin, back on fire.

Now the senior nurse on call came in, a squat and thickset man named Gabe. He paused at the door, craning his neck into the dim of the room. He wore scrubs over an old military green undershirt, its collar rimmed pink and purple with bleach stains and stretched around his neck like a yoke. Beneath the shirt, white fuzz escaped from his chest. At what he saw, he squeezed his hands to fists. The muscles of his forearms became taut as old ropes. He had tattoos here, and they ran down to the wrists. These commemorations were faded with age. They were ugly, too.

He headed toward Eden's bed no faster than a walk, leading with the forceful bludgeon of his chin. Gabe had time as a medic in the Army and years as a nurse outside it, he'd seen all sorts of guys get rejigsawed in all sorts of ways, he'd learned rushing never did any good. He stood next to Eden and studied the monitors that crowded his room.

Eden thrashed against the shift nurse and she struggled to hold him down. She wrestled him carefully, trying not to hurt him, like a hunter holds down a wounded stag before finishing it off, making sure it doesn't snap any of its points.

Gabe stopped looking at the monitors. He pulled a thick syringe from a steel drawer by the bed. He filled it with some clear juice in his pocket and told the shift nurse to hop off Eden.

She knew little about the senior nurse, just that he always volunteered for the Christmas shift. For a moment she looked back, refusing to move.

He told her again: "Go on. Get off him!"

Frightened of Gabe, she jumped from the bed.

Eden gave one hard flop, knocking every wire from his body. Gabe grabbed his throat, his hands quick as knives. Then he took the syringe and stabbed it right into my friend's failing heart.

The needle went in. The solution poured out. The heart made a fist. It punched once real hard. Eden let out a high gasp, hinting at his voice, which was swallowed long ago. Gabe held Eden's neck. The heart punched again. Slowly, Gabe eased his grip. As he did, Eden sunk into the bed.

The shift nurse got herself back together real quick. She smoothed down her blue scrubs, which were now flecked pink in the places where my friend had come off on her. Carefully, she walked around his bed, hooking the machines back up to his body. Soon the pump was droning behind him and the monitors returned to their slow beeps.

Gabe drummed his fingers at the foot of the bed. "His family here?"

"His wife went home for the holiday," said the shift nurse.

He frowned, slitting his eyes as he looked up at my friend's vitals and then back at his broken gaze. "With cardiac arrest at this stage, it's likely just a matter of time. Better give them a call."

The shift nurse walked back to her desk with the news.

Gabe walked back to his office downstairs. He hated the Christmas shift.

E den's heart tore as his family arrived at church. Mary enjoyed the service more than she'd expected. A creeping sense of well-being had found her in the pews. The feeling lingered, and afterward, as they stood in the vestibule, one of her mother's friends mentioned a Christmas party in the neighborhood. Before her mother could answer, Mary said she wanted to go.

At the party, there was a pack of children. They ran toy trucks across the carpets and played hide-and-seek among the closets and under tables. Andy chased after this pack and Mary stood beside the punch bowl, talking with the other mothers. She pretended these women didn't know about her, and they pretended back. By the time they left the party it was dark and the girl fell asleep on the car ride home. Mary pulled her floppy limbs from the backseat, carrying her into the house and up into the bed of her old room. Then, downstairs, Mary saw her mother, who stood by the answering machine, unmoving.

It flashed red with messages.

Mary pressed the play button. The youthful voice of the shift nurse came through the machine's speaker. It was contorted into a deadpan, like a dentist's reminder for a cleaning. Mary reeled against the words that came next, each one like a flashbulb going off in her face: "cardiac arrest . . . still trying to reach you, Mrs. Malcom . . . reduced brain activity . . . patient unable to sleep . . . imminent . . . imminent . . ."

Upstairs, they took Andy from her bed and drove to the airport.

Along the highway it was silent. The dashed lane markers pulsed toward them, reflecting their headlights. The green and white signs of the interstate passed above them, in a rhythm which soothed like breaking waves. Mary thought about her husband, and the word *imminent,* and maybe once this was over, once he'd gone, things would get better for her and the girl.

They'd start again, and that'd be a good thing.

Her husband dying would be a good thing.

She felt the infidelity of that thought pass between her legs and then up into her stomach in a way I knew she'd felt at least once before.

She looked out at the land along the highway and it was flattened by darkness. It spread to great distances and in them she could see the airport, the lights of its runways and towers. At first the lights seemed close, but driving proved them to be far away. And when her mother took the off-ramp toward the terminal, it was in the earliest hours of the morning. Driving in, they saw no one and continued, past the parking lots, all filled with the abandoned cars of Christmas vacationers. Then they pulled into the long and empty departures promenade.

Mary stepped from the car as it was still rolling. Her mother called after her: "If it's needed, I can put Andy on a flight so she can say goodbye to him."

Mary took a step back toward the car. She cupped her hands and placed them on the rear seat's window, peering inside. There, the girl slept in her nightgown, her hands clasped together, as if in prayer, wedged between her knees.

In the terminal, the only person Mary found was a janitor riding a miniature Zamboni, its shaggy wheel-brush rubbing moons of wax into the vast resin floor. He bumped along in his seat, the crescents of his pattern driving toward her. He shouted over the machine: "You still got a few hours till the early morning flights. Where you headed?"

"Home," she said.

Sitting on the cheap vinyl-upholstered benches, she leaned her head against her shoulder but couldn't sleep. Then she lay down on the hard resin floor. It pressed into her hip, in the same place it had pressed when she slept on the floor of her daughter's room. Soon the man on the Zamboni circled back. He stopped his machine and called down from his seat: "There's a chapel by USAir. It's unlocked and the priest leaves cots inside."

She looked up at him. "No, I'm more comfortable out here."

During the night he breathed slowly, waiting for the cockroaches to take him. Drifting, he saw flashes of when he'd first been with his wife: her sleeping in his old Mustang, it parked at Onslow Beach before they could get their own place on base, her feet in the cold beach sand when he'd come see her after evening formation, her making him dinner in the backseat of the car, peanut butter sandwiches, feeding the bread ends to the seagulls, and the seagulls perching on the hood of the Mustang, pecking the windshield for more, a quick ceremony at the justice of the peace in Jacksonville, the courthouse smelling like old carpet and forgotten paper, a meal together at Chili's afterward, and the next day, because they were now eligible, filing to move into base housing, him not returning to the barracks but waiting a week with her on the beach, a honeymoon of sorts, then their papers clearing and them moving out of the Mustang and in together.

He saw it all, and me too, and what I'd done. The pieces of that assembled and disassembled in his mind like a puzzle he hoped would stop fitting together.

And with the memory of me, the thousand

cockroach steps returned, vibrating behind him. In that sound, his feeling was reduced to a single pulsing sensation, willing the cockroaches to leave him alone. All through the night, he came and went like this. By the earliest part of the morning, just about the time Mary boarded her flight back, his mind was so far gone it tore like his heart, and the result was a schism that left less of him, but also more.

For the first time he knew it clearly: he wanted the end.

The shift nurse squeaked down the hall in her rubber-soled shoes, headed toward Eden's room. She opened the door and above his bed the bank of monitors made their noises. Before she checked them, his eyes told it all to her. They were still rheumy, slick and red, but the pupil of one was down to a pin and the pupil of the other was as wide and black as an olive. He'd had a stroke and the monitors showed that his heart was almost gone as well. He needed rest, but the body has a way of killing itself when it doesn't want to go on, and she stood over him having very unscientific thoughts about how maybe this was the right way for it to be. Maybe the body knew better than the medicine.

She sat on the edge of Eden's bed while his uneven eyes read her face, as if looking for a hidden message, scrawled in lemon juice, one that told life to be always the right choice.

He began to shiver.

From a set of drawers, she brought over a blanket. She swaddled him in it. Still, he shivered. He shivered until he stopped, and then he sweat. She pulled the blanket back a bit. The air was warm from the heater by the window and outside there was a bright moon. She shuttered

57

the blinds. Trestles of shadow fell across Eden's bed.

He never stopped looking at her.

She returned to the edge of the bed, inched next to him and placed her hand along the hem of his blanket, just below his collar, where the hairs of his chest once curled. She reached under the blanket, near the place on the bandage her finger had touched before, but now she put her whole palm on his bare skin, unworried about infection. This wouldn't matter, he was so close. One last time she wanted to know the feeling of him.

In his body she felt many different things at once. Frozen soil. The bark of a tree. Baked sand. A handful of gravel. Glass, both shattered and whole. His textures were a mosaic of many, trapped in the inches of his skin.

Her even eyes held his uneven ones as she touched him. In the space between them there was only her whispering: "If you want to go, go. But if you want to stay, sleep."

She stood from his bed, checking all the wires and hoses that connected him to the monitors above. The Snoopy tree continued to flash in the corner. She chose to leave it on, hoping its simple colors might soothe him. Then her shoes squeaked back down the corridor.

The phone at her desk rang. It was the senior nurse, Gabe. She told him about the stroke and fading vitals. "All right" was his reply.

She hung up and continued to read her magazine, but only made it through a few pages. Soon she began to wander among the empty patient rooms searching for some other way to pass the time.

H ello?" Mary called down the hall.

She'd been up most of the night and now stood at the shift nurse's desk. Sheaves of medical forms were scattered across it. She cast her eyes among them, finding her husband's name on many.

A shuffling noise came from a far room at the end of the hall. Mary walked toward it. There was a floor-to-ceiling window there, and in it, in the early morning dark, she could see the Panam Expressway and two distinct beads of traffic, one shining red and the other white, spooling and unspooling into opposite distances. Aside from the traffic, the window showed a perfect blackness. Reflected in it was the harsh glare of fluorescent bulbs shining in rows above her head, and the tired shadows of her return trip etched across her face.

She lingered on her reflection for a moment.

The shift nurse craned her head from the last door in front of the window. In her hands was another magazine. Promptly, she tossed it back through the door and took Mary down the hall to Eden's room. Inside it was dark except for the lights of the Snoopy tree. They pulsed against the monitors, IV stands and tubes, blotting colored shadows against the smooth linoleum floor.

Mary looked at the tree, not her husband.

"I thought he'd be calmed by it," said the shift nurse.

Mary smiled back, flatly, and switched on the rest of the lights in the room. Her gaze wandered over him, resting on his dark, uneven pupils and the lids of his eyes, which had become pulpy and slick. She sat quietly on the side of his bed and placed her hand on the blanket that covered him. She could feel heat coming off his body.

"Was he cold?" Mary asked.

As long as his wife was there, the shift nurse hadn't wanted to enter the room. She'd stood in the door, her hand braced against the jamb. But now she stepped toward Eden's bed, explaining: "He'd had a chill before, some fever."

The two women both rested their hands on his chest.

Eden gave no response, but turned toward the tree, the lights shining in his face.

"He needs to sleep," said the shift nurse. "His mind is very"—and she paused for the right word—"tired."

Mary looked back at her. "I'll let you know if we need anything."

The shift nurse left the room and her shoes squeaked as she walked to her desk.

Mary climbed onto the bed next to Eden. She

lay down, careful not to tug on the wires that fed in and out of his body. Against her, she could feel the warmth of him, and she remembered how he'd been in their bed: a sleeping furnace, she used to tell him. In the night, he'd roll over and throw a beefy arm or a tree trunk of a leg on her, and she'd be pinned by his weight. When the bed was cold he'd get in first, wearing nothing but his underwear or nothing at all. He'd roll around in it like a dog, heating every hidden pocket. He'd then declare the bed warm and, if she agreed, she'd climb in and let him peel off her sweats and socks. In the mornings, he'd always get up before she did. He'd run and then lift weights or box in the garage. Sometimes she'd see him returning from their bedroom window, steam tumbling from his shoulders in the cold, or she'd hear a friend of his downstairs calling him, "BASE Jump," their fists pounding the heavy bag that hung from a ceiling beam or their weights clinking in and out of the racks, gentle as teacups on saucers. She'd rise and make the bed, tucking the sheets down and finding great curled strands of his body hair between the folds. It made her feel like she slept with a barn animal.

Now, lying along the edge of his bed, she remembered all the heat of him, even though what remained was a mean little coal. "Sleep, sleep," she said, not certain which type of sleep she was urging, not certain she didn't want to sleep herself so she might wake to the cold, finding the fire in him had gone out.

Mary drifted.

Around her the room chilled. She felt him becoming heavier in the bed, relaxing, loosening, and on the backs of her eyes she could see the lights of the Snoopy tree, exploding.

Then she felt every muscle in his body go taut, lifting him. He bucked, his head thrashed, eyes both wide, pupils uneven. Behind the bed, she heard the vibrating of a cellphone. Her phone, the one she'd lost. The monitors around them beeped furiously. Every time the phone vibrated behind him, the monitors became louder and faster, until his vitals were almost a solid tone.

Then the phone stopped its vibrating. The beeping slowed. He relaxed back into the bed. His breathing calmed.

"Easy, easy," she told him, petting his hair, a thin and hard scrabble that ran in patches on his head. She watched his eyes. They frantically searched the room as if something were coming for him, but she didn't know what.

As the door opened, she climbed from the bed. The shift nurse ran in, looking him over quickly, checking his connections to the many tubes and wires, reading his vitals from the monitors above. The beeping had faded now, becoming soft. The shift nurse hurried out of the room, telling Mary that the senior nurse was on his way.

Again, she was alone with him. She knelt by his bedside, resting her cheek along the mattress's edge, her eyes running the seam of his linens and into his stare. She was ready to say goodbye, thinking of what she wanted to tell him or, if he couldn't hear it, what she wanted to tell herself.

The phone behind him vibrated quickly once more: an old voicemail.

He whimpered lowly, as both wounded animals and scared children do. His teeth chattered, as if with a fever. Then he strained his uneven eyes behind him, looking to where the vibrating noise had come from. And as Eden's mind slipped toward the horizon, Mary wondered what strange shadows it was casting.

Then she knew: it was the sound of the phone's thousand vibrations that terrified him.

It was killing him.

This wasn't his body shutting itself down in some physiological self-destruct. Her husband couldn't sleep because she'd forgotten her phone in his room.

She could leave it there.

All the suffering would end. No one would know she was the one who'd done it. And what would she be killing? The lump of flesh in front of her wasn't a husband, it certainly wasn't the famed BASE Jump, all of that ended in a flash three years ago along a strip of road in the Hamrin Valley. She wasn't even sure that leaving the phone there could be called killing. Events in motion would simply be left in motion.

But she couldn't.

If she'd had that in her to do, she would've done it a long time ago. So she stood from the side of his bed, smoothed down the front of her shirt and took a few breaths. "Okay," she said, hating him in that broken way we reserve for those we truly love.

She walked behind his bed, unplugged her phone and slid it into her pocket. She also unplugged the lights from the Snoopy tree. She shut the door behind her, and as night turned to morning outside, his room remained completely dark.

When Mary stepped behind Eden's bed, he worried that the army of cockroaches would consume her. But when she returned unharmed, he thought she had a strength, one that despite all he'd become he'd never known in himself. He watched her as she unplugged the Snoopy tree and walked toward the door, and then behind her, from a crack in the wall, came the lone cockroach. As she flipped off the light switch, the cockroach looked back at him.

Then it followed his wife into the hallway and out of the darkness.

Left alone, Eden slept.

If you asked either of them how they met, you were likely to get one of three answers. If you asked Eden, and Mary wasn't there, he'd tell you that they met in high school. He'd explain how they'd run in the same crowds and how he'd pursued her among other, lesser suitors, and you'd be left with midwestern images of varsity letter jackets, Dairy Queens and make-out parties. You'd also be left with the strange sense that he, still in his teen years, could size up what was barely a woman and decide that he could do what you couldn't as a grown man: know that she was wife material and land her. Now if you asked Mary, and Eden wasn't there, she'd tell you that they'd known each other in high school but started dating afterward, and even then things became serious only once he got stationed at Camp Lejeune and she had to decide whether to leave him or come along. The last iteration of their story, and the one that was closest to the truth, was the version you'd get if you asked and they were together. One of them, the one that was feeling the most considerate toward the other, would take up the question as though it were his or her turn with the dishes and say flatly: "We're from the same hometown."

I say this was the nearest version to the truth because the truth as I saw it, as their friend, was that they ran into each other because of the town. When I say they ran into each other, I don't mean like they bumped into each other, I mean they were both running away when they met and these forces of flight played matchmaker surer than any homeroom class or semiformal dance.

To Eden and Mary, home seemed like a quiet type of terrorism: courses at the local community college, part-time jobs that took none of their skill but all of their energy, friends they'd had their whole lives with the promise that they'd have no others. For both of them home was a place long defined not by who lived there but by who'd left: for her a father who'd died young, for him an aunt who raised him, dying all along from her own slow sickness. Together Eden and Mary ran from all this, and it's difficult not to fall in love with someone you're on the run with. But you stop eventually, and then—

I think I met them right about the time they were hitting the *and then*. He and I were team leaders in the same platoon, corporals, which meant we were a couple of years older than the guys in our teams and already had a deployment under our belts. It also meant we'd come in the Corps before the war started, which, to the younger guys, made us seem like that old and strange breed of regular who soldiered for soldiering's sake. And maybe we did—we didn't know yet.

We were both coming to the ends of our first four-year enlistments, and we were both trying to decide if we wanted four more. It was natural we became friends.

Whether we reenlisted or not, our infantry battalion was getting ready for its next deployment. This meant lots of training at night—driving at night, shooting at night, patrolling at night— once we got good at something during the day, our lieutenant would inevitably gather us all together and tell us we'd now have to get good at it at night. I often wondered why we didn't just learn to do everything at night in the first place.

We would deploy in the winter, and all through the summer, when the days were long, we trained like this. The lieutenant would let us off work early at 1500 and tell us to be back at 2100, when it finally got dark. He'd explain that we weren't really working any harder. He'd say that if we didn't train nights we'd have to work until 1800, but now we'd come back in and be off at midnight. "Three hours is fuckin' three hours," he'd tell us. But even he must have known this was bullshit because after that he'd say: "So no fuckin' complaints," and they only said that when there was something to complain about.

But when Eden invited me to his house for dinner and I met Mary, I never complained about working late again.

My first time over, it was a Tuesday. He'd roasted a duck, and I remember thinking, Who roasts a duck on a Tuesday? We ate at a table she'd set in their kitchen, but she had only salad. She wore her gym clothes, and we wore our uniforms, all of us smelling faintly of sweat. She was a vegetarian, fish sometimes but definitely not duck, and she told me this as I passed her the platter with the duck on it. I set the platter down, and as I did I saw her looking at my hand. I had a scar across my knuckles and she asked whether I boxed, because Eden liked to box.

"No, it's an old tattoo," I told her. "I got it removed."

"What was it?"

"USMC."

She gave me a confused look, as if wondering why I removed that tattoo off my hand while I was still in the Corps.

"I got it when I was sixteen," I explained. "My parents didn't approve."

Eden laughed at me a little bit. His arms were covered in tribal designs. Spiderwebs burst from his elbows, and skulls hung here and there. He wasn't halfway through his twenties and already he'd need another body if he wanted to ink any more of his story into it.

"So you always wanted to do this?" she asked me.

Eden interrupted before I could answer: "He's going to extend for our next deployment." I hadn't signed the papers yet, but he was right, they'd already been drawn up.

She looked at her husband and didn't say anything. He'd yet to reenlist. I knew that and knew she didn't want to talk about his choice to stay or go in front of me.

I answered her: "Yeah, I think I always knew."

"Show him your tattoo," Eden told her. Then he said to me, as if revealing some secret of his wife's: "She was about sixteen too."

Mary pulled her dark ponytail to the side, so it hung over her shoulder. On the groove in the back of her neck was what looked like a small group of blue freckles. "Andromeda," she said. "When I was a kid, it rose out my bedroom window." I must have been looking at her with a stupid expression, because she added: "Andromeda's a constellation."

I nodded as though I already knew that, but I saw nothing of a constellation in this pattern. To me, it was only a smattering of blue against her very white skin. Still, I wanted to trace my fingers between these stars, connecting, I don't know what. Maybe that was the point.

I said nothing, and for a moment everything became awkward among the three of us. Then my friend stamped hard on the floor. "Fuckers!" he said and lifted his foot. Crushed beneath it, and smeared into the shag carpet, was a pair of cockroaches.

"Did you have to do that?" asked Mary, wincing as she scooped the mess up with her napkin.

"Christ, I hate bugs," he said, looking at me.

Mary tossed her napkin in the trash, washed her hands and sat back down. When we finished our meal she offered to do the dishes, but he said we'd do them. And it was in little ways like cleaning up the crushed cockroaches and doing the dishes that I noticed they were always kind to each other. She left the table and walked into the back of the house. We finished the dishes, and as I turned off the faucet, I noticed the shower going in another room. My eyes wandered in that direction as if imagining the water against her nakedness, running on her neck. I must have looked for too long because Eden said: "Yep, I'd think you were weird if you didn't."

I felt my blood go warm and it spread from my stomach into my limbs, him knowing what I felt toward her before I did.

"C'mon," he said and nodded at the door.

We walked out through the garage, the two

of us. Here, an Everlast heavy bag hung from a chain. I hit it once as hard as I could. Eden smiled at me and we drove back into work, where we'd shoot all through the night.

On the range, machine guns fired long bursts, and when the guns went high, the tracers cut red incisions into the sky until they disappeared, and when the guns went low, the tracers cartwheeled into the earth, starting fires in the brush. From our shoulders we shot rockets, and when they missed their targets, they slammed into the ground, throwing up great fountains of earth and then dust. And when they hit, they hit the steel hulls of old tanks and showered sparks into the darkness and brush, and this caused more fires, and soon the fires were so many that we had to stop shooting and wait until they burned out. So we waited and it grew later than midnight.

I didn't mind the waiting because I did it with Eden, and we sat on the ground in the darkness. "Fucking look at it burn," he said. And I could see the firelight reflecting off his smile. For a while neither of us spoke. We were too tired. Then he said: "She's mad at me, you know. She's teaching two, sometimes three classes a day at that gym. I told her it's too much and she needs to quit, so she's mad at me."

"So what if it's too much?" I said. Anyways, it didn't sound like much.

He glanced at me, making some invisible

judgment, then he added: "We're trying, you know, and having trouble."

I stood and shook my legs. They'd fallen asleep. I also wanted to see if the fires were dying, but they weren't, they were spreading. Then I looked down at him, and he was already looking up at me.

"So you're not going to reenlist? You'll stay back here and get out," I said.

"I don't think I could do it all again with a kid back home."

I nodded.

"But we're having trouble," he added.

I sat down next to him and leaned back, searching the night sky for Andromeda, and I think he knew I was searching for it, but I don't think he cared because he knew I couldn't find it and he'd learned how to a long time ago.

Then the stars disappeared and the fires went out.

It had started to rain.

Eden woke up and then he became awake. He was still in the hospital. After the stroke, everything had been reorganized. Some things were gone, but others had been added. His vision was gone. Now there were just the blurs that separated darkness from light. Lying there, awake, he watched the bright blur of morning. In that blur were memories, a head full of them. Each was only a speck, but they were like pieces of sand seen so close that they appeared as entire planets. The time he'd spent with her in the Mustang at Onslow Beach became a universe to him. Her breath had smelled like the peanut butter in their sandwiches, he remembered that, and also that she'd worn the same bra for nearly a week. It was black. Its lace was rough under his fingers and he touched it whenever he could, reading her body like braille.

His wife.

As he lay there, he could smell her near him. Soap and water. She always had a way of saving him. He looked toward the lightest part of the room, by the window, where he knew she slept on the couch.

How long had she been there?

A man should be able to look down on his

wife sleeping, he thought. Look down, close his eyes and smell her. And he could now do some of these things, and in them, he felt himself returning. Other memories returned, too. He thought of the cockroaches from before. They seemed like a dream and his terror an embarrassment.

I know what's real now, he told himself.

Through the springs in his bed, he felt Mary's feet plant on the floor.

He could feel so much.

This too was new.

The light dimmed by the window, she was blocking it, standing over him. What are you looking at? he thought. He could feel the clean softness of sheets pulled to his neck, and he could feel his skin, tight and crumpled like wax paper against the bones and muscles of his face. He could feel her breath, her lips moving against his cheek as she spoke soundlessly to him, the heavy curtain of her hair mixing with the stubborn and bristled crust of his hair. She kept her lips moving, whispering so low her voice couldn't be heard. Then he felt a great vibration from the other side of the room. He thought it was a door slamming, but he couldn't hear it. Her lips kept moving.

Like prayers, the rhythm of her words never stopped.

He could hear none of it.

He couldn't hear.

A rush of anxiety welled up in him, crashed and then spilled like a silent wave of nothing. For there was nothing he wanted to see or hear. If he could've heard, the nurses would've told him he was blind. If he could've seen, the nurses would've written words to tell him he was deaf. I won't be afraid, he promised himself. I will be bigger than everyone else.

I will be dead.

I will be on this earth closer to death than anyone and knowing what only the dead know. That is something, he thought, to know what only the dead know. And what is that? All they know is they were once alive, and are dead only because of it.

Through the springs in his bed, he felt the door slam again. Then he felt fast little footsteps working their way around the room. It was so clear to him. He could imagine the entire room. How could you let her see me like this, he thought. Then he felt a soft hand with narrow bones petting his head, carefully, and then another smaller and more delicate hand.

Andy's.

The small hand wouldn't quite open and it rested on him in a little fist, clutching at itself. Then he felt the fast little footsteps move away from him.

Mary shouldn't have brought her for this, he

thought. Was it so important for the girl to have some last memory of him, even if it was this one? Years before, on the news, he recalled seeing a certain report of a school shooting. As the children had walked out of their classrooms hand in hand, a policeman had the presence of mind to tell them to shut their eyes so they wouldn't see their dead classmates spread out in the hallways and gymnasium. The policeman had been hailed as a hero for sparing the children that sight.

He wanted to be like that policeman.

He could feel the sweat coming off him as he lay there, the sting of it in the open wounds around his neck and sides, and the sheet getting wet and sticking to his back, also his heart thrumming against his chest, too big and too strong to just die. He felt like his heart was burying him, pounding him deeper and deeper into the bed, so deep that eventually the sheets would envelop him, closing invisibly over his head like mud-waters.

Why did she let Andy see him like this, naked and disfigured?

He worked to breathe slowly, but still his heart pounded. He shut his eyes, counted to one hundred, recited the Lord's Prayer. The pounding kept up. The sensation was familiar, one he'd felt often enough before. It was how it'd been after his first deployment, when they'd tried to conceive the girl.

Eden didn't think trying in the old way would help, but Mary did and she drove them to their old place at Onslow Beach. It was winter and the parking lot was empty. Seagulls flew overhead and they looked black against the sun. The seagulls also walked on the dunes and here they looked white. She parked the Mustang with its fender to a break in the dunes, looking out at the ocean. Near the shore the wind chopped whitecaps into the waves, but farther out the wind wasn't as strong and the water was very smooth. On the ocean there were a few big ships and they were distant enough to look like they stood still, even though they moved fast and heavy as big ships do.

When she turned the ignition off, he didn't say anything and it was quiet between them. The heat wasn't on and soon it escaped the car and the air became cold inside it. She became cold and frustrated that he wouldn't touch her. So she turned the car on again and reached into the backseat for a bag of bread ends she'd brought. She stepped outside and fed the seagulls while the car heated up.

He watched her from the passenger seat. She walked up to the dunes with the bag and the seagulls that had been there flew off. They circled in the sky where the sun was and again they looked black against it. Then she began to throw pieces of the bread in the air. A few of the seagulls were able to catch the bread in this way, but it was hard to do and most couldn't manage. So the bread fell into the sand and soon the seagulls gathered around her. She laughed as they came close, pecking at her feet with their yellow bills and white necks. He looked into the sky and he could no longer see the black silhouettes of any seagulls, even those that could catch the bread had chosen to do what was easy and gather around her.

Soon the bag was empty and she came back through the dunes toward the Mustang. The wind on the beach had blown across her face, reddening her cheeks. She climbed into the driver's seat. The car had been warm for a while and she was very cold now, and she said as much, hoping he might warm her.

He pressed her hands between his two. And hers were soft and so cold he wondered if the narrow bones in them might snap. She leaned into him and breathed warmly toward his neck. He began to feel as though he wasn't warming her, but that she was making him cold. The curtain of her hair was now very close to his face and he could smell her smell. He couldn't tell the difference between her hands and his, they both felt numb to him. She pulled back for a moment. He felt his heart eating at his chest in a way that had become more and more familiar in the many months since he'd returned home. She took off her sweater and beneath it she wore the black lace bra from before, from when it had been easy for him. He touched her, and she flinched against his cold hands. Knowing she'd done this, she leaned into him, encouraging him. He could feel the blood in all his body collapsing onto his heart as he ran his fingers over the rough lace that cupped her chest. She reached after him, hoping to find something there. But what he had for her was unmoving and cold. Still she climbed on him, becoming warmer herself and trying to warm him under her. She went on with it until her face was pink and sweat beaded beneath her eyes. But he had become too cold to make anything of it, so he pushed her off him. She sat back in the driver's seat and turned off the Mustang.

Neither spoke for a time. Without her on him, he felt his body returning and she dressed and put on her sweater. Then she told him: "I'll be with you for as long as it takes."

"What did I lose over there?" he asked, staring at the ocean and the unmoving ships on it.

"Nothing you'll find by going back," she said, knowing his mind.

He exchanged a look with her, unsure what to say. Then one of the seagulls landed on the hood of the Mustang. It pecked at the windshield wipers, wanting something more. They had nothing else to give, so the two of them left and went home.

t was now the day after Christmas and the late afternoon sky was sharp and blue, filled with a cold wind. Dressed in sweats and a wool peacoat, Mary stood outside the hospital's automatic doors. She snubbed out her second cigarette and put the butt in her pocket. There was nowhere else to put it. Above her, streetlamps already glowed, anticipating the night, but daylight lingered, keeping the lamps dim. She walked beneath the lamps and along a cement path that wound through a grass field and to a dormitory, built long and low, like a bedridden skyscraper.

Andy had arrived early that afternoon. She'd visited her mother at the hospital before, but she'd been a baby the last time she saw Eden. Mary, whose instinct was to protect her daughter from certain memories, had been overruled by her mother, who insisted the girl be put on a plane for a final visit. And so late that day Mary stood next to Eden's bed with her daughter. She had told Andy to put a hand on his chest. Andy hadn't wanted to, but she did. And that was it. Between mother and daughter, at least one of them had managed to tell him goodbye.

Now Andy napped in the dormitory room.

Mary climbed a single flight of stairs. At her

door, she slowly slid the key into the lock and eased the latch open. She slipped into the space that was both kitchen and living room. The last of the light cast pinstripes through the blinds, landing on the sofa, where Andy slept under a mound of covers. Mary perched up on a barstool at the kitchen counter. She reached into a fruit bowl piled to the brim with unopened mail. She took a handful and began to thumb through it, bills mostly: insurance claims, utilities and rent she still paid for base housing, phone payments and the rest of it. There was also junk mail, solicitations and scams that had been sent to her address at the burn center. Mary often wondered what sort of a son-of-a-bitch would send junk mail to an address with "Family Support Facility, Burn Center" in it. But it wasn't one person. It was many. She imagined the hundreds of them at their desks, databases opened, pecking her name and the words *Burn Center* at their keyboards, over and over.

She threw the mail back into the fruit bowl. She'd finish her bills later and knew she was fortunate. Money was one of the few things she didn't have to worry about. The insurance had paid out plenty.

She worried about Eden, though. Gabe, the old nurse with the faded tattoos, had told her to head back to her room and get some rest. These last couple of days he'd taken a personal interest in

Eden and he'd promised to call with the news they were all waiting for. And even though Gabe had said he'd call, she still couldn't sleep. So she watched her daughter sleep.

The sun set and filled the dormitory room with a brief type of orange light, like a liquid, and then darkness. Quickly it became cold and Andy began to kick away her blankets, as if she wanted the cold. Still her mother knew better, and knew the girl needed rest. She crossed the room and pulled the blankets back over Andy's shoulders and tucked them behind her. Her daughter was warm again, pinned beneath the blankets, and for as long as Mary could she would make sure the girl slept.

Eden and Mary had tried many times before, but after that time at the beach he wouldn't try again. Instead, he began to throw himself into his training: he practiced his *shukran*s and *as salaam alaikum*s, he drilled the privates in small-unit tactics, he held inspections without anyone asking him to. I noticed the change in him even though I didn't understand it. He also stopped complaining about our night training. He no longer complained about the lieutenant either, and he didn't seem to mind that we'd finish our days at 1500 and then have to come back at 2100. In fact, he didn't even go home during this time. He just stayed at work, waiting for it to get dark.

Now there was no dinner for me to be invited to. But it wasn't the dinner I missed, it was her. So at 1500, while he stayed at work, I'd go exercise at her gym. I knew her class schedule and I'd make sure to be finishing about the same time she was. She'd stand by the door of the wood-floored aerobics studio and as each of her students left, she'd thank and encourage them, as if she were a minister after Sunday services. I'd walk by and she'd smile at me, too. Sometimes she'd ask about the training we had planned that night, but she never asked as though she were interested, she asked as though she were fact-checking what Eden had told her.

After a while, she must have understood that I waited for her. Even on days when her class schedule changed, I'd finish my workouts when she finished hers. For weeks niceties and nothing else passed between us. Then, one night after her late class, as she let her students go, I smiled at her as I usually did. But she didn't seem to notice. From one of the gym's mirrors, I watched as she cleaned up the equipment in her studio with quick little movements. Set across her face was a vacant look with some type of worry knitting her eyebrows close, and after I showered and walked out of the gym I found her alone in the parking lot smoking a cigarette.

She still wore her sweaty clothes. When I stepped outside, she cupped her hand around the cigarette, hiding its burn, but when she saw it was me, she kept on smoking. I didn't know that she smoked and it seemed strange that she'd do it here, outside the gym. An awkwardness passed between us and she asked if I was going back to work. I didn't answer her question, but asked if she had another cigarette. She offered one and we stood together.

"It's an old habit," she finally said. "I quit before I married him."

I lit my cigarette from the tip of hers, but said nothing. Her hair was up and I thought about the tattoo on the back of her neck, and this made me think about the stars, so I looked at the sky, but they weren't out. A few clouds and a late sunset still hid them.

She inhaled off her cigarette and spoke, exhaling smoke: "He told me about a course in Maine he has to go to. Do all of you have to go?"

The course was in survival, evasion, resistance, escape—SERE school—where we'd learn what to do if we ever became prisoners. It was required training for those who'd committed to the next deployment. I didn't know that included him, but I knew to tread carefully in what I said to her. "I'm not sure who else is signed up, but I have to go."

"It's always *have to* with you all, as if you have no choice, as if you've conveniently forgotten you volunteered for all this." She snubbed her cigarette out on her running shoe and lit another as though it were some act of revenge. "You ever think that once or even never was enough?"

I began to smoke quickly, wanting to finish and leave. I flicked my cigarette across the parking lot, toward the Dumpsters. She touched my arm. "Have one more?" she asked.

There was a weight to her eyes, like gravity holding me in place. I took another, and as I did she sat on the asphalt with her back against the wall of the gym. I sat next to her and the ground still trapped the fading day's warmth.

"Going back a second time, are you more or less scared?" she asked.

"It's just different," I replied. "The first time, I wanted to go. Now I need to."

"Needing something is scarier," she said.

We both smoked and looked up at the darkening sky. I tried to remember the strange shape of Andromeda dotted on the back of her neck. She looked off in what I thought was the constellation's direction. I followed her stare with my own, but could see nothing except the nonsense of rising stars.

She turned toward me as if she might say something else, or try to teach me how to find the constellation. The thought of saying or doing more with her made a coward of me. I looked at my watch and told her I needed to get back to work.

After Mary returned to the dormitory, Eden lay awake by himself. A few minutes later, the door swung open just a crack. He could feel this through the vibrations in his bedsprings and he could feel the footsteps that came toward him, heavy and even. He knew this was Gabe, the one who'd grabbed him by the throat before. He felt his heart eating a hole in his chest in the familiar way, and he could feel currents of his blood moving to the center of him.

He was afraid of Gabe.

But there was a lot Eden didn't know about him. For instance, he didn't know Gabe's shift had ended hours ago and that he stayed on, wanting to be there for the end. Eden didn't know he reminded Gabe of his friends, guys from another war, where he'd first learned to fix men. Not permanent fixes, but the small repairs that would buy a man the time he needed to get on a helicopter and fly to a place where real repairs could be made. In his war, Gabe had learned almost all there was to know about buying a broken body time. Chest compress, clotting agent, tourniquet, nasopharyngeal tube, all of it the vocabulary of saved moments. Over the years of Gabe's war, and after, he'd watched the minutes he bought for his friends turn into sentences of too many hours, days and months. Soon he learned it wasn't too little time that was the enemy but too much. For in the end, it was time that turned all his friends' fractures to breaks. And for his friends, the moments from their saving to their ends became a list of torments caused by him.

Now all Gabe hoped to bring was speed.

Eden knew none of this, but he did know Gabe's heavy footsteps and, as the old nurse hovered over him, Eden could smell the faint alkaline odor of his sweat. Eden felt vulnerable, trapped in his own body, with no voice to sound the alarm of his suffering. He'd been vulnerable like this before, during the three weeks of our training at SERE school, where we'd learned how an imprisoned man survives. As Eden lay in his bed those memories came back. First the old noises echoed in his deaf ears: sounds of the camp we'd lived in, an invention of the training. Each man was kept alone in a cage. The floors of the cages were dirt, but the course was up in Maine and it was fall, so most days the rains turned the floors to mud. Eden remembered the wetness of the mud and how it stuck to his prisoner's pajamas, recycled scrubs donated from a state sanitarium. He also remembered the insects that occasionally crawled across that floor and how they terrified him. Without warning we were taken from our cages and questioned, but crueler than this were the hours left with our thoughts and anxieties. Through days of simulation, steel locks slammed against wood doors as each of us was hauled off for interrogation and returned. Clipped questions came from instructors who played the role of our interrogators, some of them acting the part and others indulging in it. The noise of prisoners answering questions was ceaseless. It ran into each night, punctuated only by the hollow clap of an open palm striking one of our faces when a question wasn't answered, or was answered poorly. These strikes were designed not to break bone or skin, but to sting and remind.

Soon our greatest struggle became unrelated to our interrogations and beatings. The struggle for us became one of holding on to what was real, and of understanding what wasn't. On the first day of the course, before the camp simulation began, the instructors gathered us in a classroom and warned how reality would slip easily from us in the camp. They drew a diagram on the board:

|   | 1 | 2 | 3 | 4 | 5 |
|---|---|---|---|---|---|
| 1 | A | B | C/K | D | E |
| 2 | F | G | H | I | J |
| 3 | L | M | N | O | P |
| 4 | Q | R | S | T | U |
| 5 | V | W | X | Y | Z |

This grid was tap code, a tool we could use to communicate from cell to cell, one that would help us hold on to our reality. Communication, we were told, would be our only defense against the stresses of isolation and confinement. Without it we didn't stand a chance of passing the course and, if we were ever taken prisoner, without it we'd lose our minds. To teach us how the grid worked, the instructors had us all bang out a single word: 5, 1 / 3, 3 / 4, 1—END. This was our safe word. If we banged it out a few times our training would be over. We'd fail the course, but as we were told: "You'll get a hot meal, a cot, and a ticket home." What was left unsaid was that we'd be taken off the next deployment, too.

We were two weeks into the course when

Eden tapped out those three letters. It wasn't the interrogations, sleep deprivation, or hunger that made him do it. Instead, it was a bit of cruelty on the part of one of the instructors and a small betrayal by me.

I'd had three interrogations the day it happened. The sessions had been long, but I couldn't say how long. I tried to keep track of the time by looking at my interrogator's watch, a simple stainless-steel Seiko on a brown leather band. When I could, I'd glance at his wrist. But whenever he left the room and returned, it seemed his watch had been set forward or back to confuse me. Soon, I had become loopy from cold and hunger, and my interrogator, seeing this, became dangerously kind, offering me a Styrofoam cup of chicken broth. He asked how the living conditions were and if there was anything that could be done to improve them. I thought of Eden. In the past few days, he'd taken to tapping: 2, 1 / 5, 4 / 2, 2—BUG. He'd tap it over and over when in the night he'd feel the insects crawling through the mud floor of his cell. It'd been a few taps at first, but now it'd become relentless, running straight through until morning. Soon the fifteen others in our camp lost patience with him and their tapped replies of SHUT UP could be heard mixing with his panicked taps of BUG, BUG, BUG. I told the interrogator this. I explained my friend's phobia to him, and that we prisoners would be more cooperative if we could get his tapping to stop. Perhaps they could put a plywood board on the floor of Eden's cell. I wanted to be helpful. I wanted to negotiate something better for my friend.

I wanted another cup of chicken broth.

The interrogator put a blanket over my shoulders. "I'm glad to know all this," he said as he brought me the cup of broth I'd wanted. Then he left me alone to drink it, and to warm under the blanket. As I sipped the second cup, I noticed it was saltier, as if it'd come from the bottom of the pot, and as I drank I knew I'd traded something for it.

That night, under the rows of floodlights, I slept on the mud floor of my cell. Through its bars, I saw the interrogator who I'd spoken to before. He walked across the camp with a glass pickle jar tucked beneath his arm. It slithered with every type of insect you could imagine.

Eden was sleeping when the interrogator opened the small door to his cell. He set the jar inside and shackled the lock back on the cage. Eden sat up. The interrogator smiled at him, checked his Seiko and said: "Just a few hours till morning."

Then he left.

Our cells weren't tall enough to stand in, and that jar was wedged right between Eden's legs.

The hundred insects swirled around the jar, pressing against the glass, millimeters from Eden's groin. They climbed on each other as he imagined they would climb on him, all poking legs and black mouths. He tried to crawl into a far corner, but there were no far corners. He tried to press the jar through the cell bars, but it was too wide. He kicked his feet at the bars, trying to break the door off, but the steel lock was too strong.

Then he began to tap. But he didn't tap BUG, he tapped END. Over and over. END, END, END. I panicked too, not because I'd betrayed Eden's fear to our interrogator, but because if he quit I'd deploy without my friend. I began to tap over him, nonsensically banging like an ape in a cage, which perhaps I was at that moment. Soon others joined, organizing on instinct, and the commotion spread. But through it, I could still hear the one thread of Eden's tapping, straining to be heard: 5, 1 / 3, 3 / 4, 1—END, END, END. All he wanted was to quit the course, but I wouldn't let him. I thought eventually he might scream, but he didn't.

Instead the sound of shattering glass came from his cell, and then silence.

The insects crawled over him and burrowed into the mud. A few minutes later a group of instructors took him from his cage.

The next morning he was brought back to camp.

His hands were bandaged from where the glass had cut them. He could've quit. There would've been no shame in it, but he stayed, and when the course finished a week later, his hands had begun to heal. For graduation there was a small ceremony and each of us was given a manila folder with a certificate of course completion. In Eden's folder that one interrogator had slipped inside his Seiko.

At the graduation party afterward all the instructors attended, except for that one. As Eden drank Guinness at the bar, I thought about telling him how I'd confessed his phobia, and how I'd done it for a cup of chicken broth. Then I saw his wrist. Proudly, he wore the watch on its leather band. At that moment, I decided not to tell him. I didn't think there was much point to it. He'd shown those assholes he wouldn't quit.

But lying in his hospital bed Eden now wondered about that watch. He wondered about the leather strap that eventually became familiar, dimpled in one place by him and in another by the instructor who'd given it to him. He imagined the watch at his bedside, or maybe it'd burned up when we hit the pressure plate in the Hamrin. He remembered how the second hand circled its face, sweeping smoothly and never ticking, the minutes passing to days. But he had no idea how time passed now. All he knew was that there was too much of it.

He could still feel Gabe in the room. And he began what I'd spoiled for him those years ago in the camp, he clacked his teeth together and tapped out the words: END, END, END.

By the time we got back from SERE school, Mary knew about Eden's reenlistment papers. We wouldn't deploy for another three months, and he wouldn't take his oath until a couple after that, but the papers were there. He'd committed.

I wondered how she took the news.

I assumed this meant they were putting their family plans on hold, but I wasn't sure. I didn't want to ask him and I kept away from her gym.

But then I got the chance to do something for her.

We were scheduled to deploy in the new year, and the afternoon before the long Columbus Day weekend the entire battalion was herded into the base theater. All through the weeks before, everyone had been traveling, finishing training courses here and there, but for this briefing no one could be absent. Nearly a thousand of us filled up the theater. There were reunions taking place in the rows of red felt seats. A lot of us hadn't seen each other for weeks. Up front, a movie screen was hidden by long curtains with a heavy hem. A large pair of Comedy and Tragedy masks crowned the stage, and a lance corporal, compact and Latina, stood beneath it. She looked out over the crowd and spoke into a microphone, her nervous voice breaking into an accent and her words barely traveling.

*"Speak up, picante!"* screamed someone in the back.

Laughter rippled across the crowd. A first sergeant trolled the aisles searching for the voice. He had a tight-set jaw, flat head like an anvil and hair trimmed like a strip of putting green.

The lance corporal turned red and smoothed down the sides of her hair, which ran solid black into a bun on the back of her head. She fiddled with the microphone's collar. Volume violently returned and her slight movements boomed over the crowd.

"Can you hear that better?" she asked.

Again from the back came a shout: *"Picante!"* Again the first sergeant moved after the voice, but now there were a couple of diversionary shouts: *"Picante!"* *"Picante!"* rising from different places in the crowd. It became quiet. The first sergeant stopped looking, but stood in the back of the theater, holding his gaze among the rows, waiting for who would try next.

The lance corporal continued: "Beneath your chairs you will find Form SGLV 8286." She rattled off the alphanumeric designator as *sig-luve eighty-two eight-six,* demonstrating a bureaucrat's flair for pronouncing any combination of letters and numbers as if it were a word. "Fill this sheet out accurately and in black ink. If you make a mistake do not try to change it, come to the stage and I'll give you a new copy. You can turn in the form today or, if you need more time, you can mail it to the address listed in Section M."

"*What's the form for?*" came another shout. The first sergeant flinched in the back row, making a move toward the voice until some part of him registered the question as legitimate.

"This is your Servicemembers' Group Life Insurance," said the lance corporal. "If anything happens to you, the government will pay out four hundred K to your family or whoever else you deem fit."

"What does *deem fit* mean?" asked another voice in the crowd. The first sergeant moved again, but stopped himself.

"Whoever you choose," she replied.

"How about my dog?" asked someone else. The first sergeant started out for the voice.

"Good question," said the lance corporal. "If you want to leave it to your dog, you can." Again, the first sergeant stopped himself.

Most everyone had begun to carefully look over their forms. Eden sat next to me and I noticed he wasn't doing anything. His form was blank. He saw me looking and said: "You interested in being roommates when we come back?"

"Can't be that bad," I said.

"Bad enough."

"She really doesn't want you to deploy, huh?"

He shook his head.

"And the baby?" I asked.

"That's what she needs."

Before I could say anything else to him, another shout came from behind us: *"What's your address, picante?"*

A flash of something registered with the first sergeant and he tore down one of the theater's side aisles, grabbing a skinny private in a headlock. He dragged the kid through the red vinyl swing doors at the back of the theater and into the lobby, where on movie night they sold Jujyfruits, Raisinets and popcorn.

Everyone went back to their work. What we each put down was personal, and perfectly diminishing, the secret or not so secret truth of who you love most placed on a form. But Eden didn't write anything. He left the form blank and slipped it into his cargo pocket to be mailed in later. Then he stood to walk out the back of the theater. As he did, he turned to me and said: "If you'd let me quit that night, I'd be stuck back here."

I looked up at him, but didn't speak.

Neither did he, but I think this was his way of thanking me.

Once he left, I listed Mary as the recipient of

my four hundred K. Even then, I knew whatever happened to me would likely happen to him. And if he wouldn't take care of her, I would make her the secret on my form.

It was early in the morning, still night really, and Mary couldn't sleep so she took a shower. Just as she turned the water off, the phone rang. She cursed under her breath, clutched her bathrobe across her chest and rushed into the den. On the sofa, Andy was still asleep and stirred while her mother dripped puddles onto the cheap shag carpet. On the phone's other end was Gabe. His voice rattled like gravel in a can: "He's having some trouble and we're worried about another seizure."

"What's he doing?" she asked; her voice was flat.

"We're not sure. His vitals are steady and there's no irregular brain activity, but he's thrashing in his bed and clacking his teeth together. It's wearing him out. I want to put him on a pretty strong sedative, but I'll need you to come sign some consent forms first."

She looked across the room. Andy was up, rubbing little fists in her eyes. Normally, Mary would've left straightaway. She would've hung up the phone and run to the hospital's main building. But that was a long time ago. Now she felt worn out and, though she'd never say it, hopeful that this was the end.

"Give me a minute," she replied and hung up.

There was a twenty-four-hour daycare where she could leave Andy. She started to dress her daughter, but the girl wanted to dress herself. Still, Mary insisted on brushing both their hair. Mary set the brush back in the bathroom. Then she dropped Andy off at the daycare, and when she did the girl cried.

Outside, a thin haze, like a frost, still hung over everything. It was now early morning and cold. The main hospital building rose above her, a column of glass and steel. In the haze it gleamed artificially, a soft coronet rested around each light. She walked through the sliding double doors and inside everything was bright and quiet. The receptionist sat bunkered behind her desk and paid no notice as Mary passed into an empty elevator. She rode up four floors and then cut down the hallways, arriving at Eden's door, still sniffing from the cold as warmth returned to her cheeks.

The room was dim and lit only by a corner lamp. Her husband's eyes were open but flittering, their rims red and pulpy as they looked at the lamp. The sheets on his bed had been pulled loose and his neck rocked slightly as he breathed. Before he'd always looked bad, but contained: tucked neatly under his sheets, his burns covered, his eyes either open—staring at nothing—or closed as he slept. Now, he was still alive but

106

uncontained and trembling. These hundred small electrocutions hinted at a migration that had begun in his body, one taking him away from life. As prepared as she felt to let him go, and as much as she wanted that final release for him, and for herself, she now felt a desperate want for him to hold on.

She sat on the side of his bed, shut her eyes and placed her hand on his head as though her touch could pull the darkness from him like venom through a wound. Then she noticed a sweet and stale smell, like the wet cigarettes she kept in the can under her mother's house. She looked up and Gabe had returned.

His thick arms worked above her, fields of black hair combing their backs like a crop in the wind. He continued to work, hanging IV bags from a stand with his stumpy fingers. He switched out Eden's fluids and there was a gentle elegance to his movements, one that belied the grim purpose in all his work. Finished, he wrapped the expended bags in their cords, and placed them into a red biohazard bin, reaching to the bottom so that the noise of them falling wouldn't disturb his patient, or her.

Even as Gabe tried to be quiet, my friend started clacking his teeth and banging his head against his pillow. It began slowly and with a very deliberate rhythm.

Mary put a hand on his shoulder. "Shhh, you're okay," she whispered.

Eden kept at it, the muscles in his neck straining as his pace quickened.

"Shhh," she said again and looked up at Gabe, who crossed the room and pressed a button above the bed. Then he stood over Eden, checking the IV bags he'd just hooked up and the bank of monitors.

"Weak vitals but nothing erratic," Gabe told her. He looked down at his patient with a mechanic's interest. Eden's eyes were wide open now, but his lids were swollen like the edges of a gash and his irises were so faded and yellowed they looked like old bones. He chomped his teeth in a rhythm, but to Gabe and Mary it was an unintelligible one.

Gabe did nothing but watch. "He's been going like this for hours," he said. "It's hard on him."

She nodded.

"I can give him some strong stuff. It'll make this whole thing easier."

"So he's going then?" she asked.

"I can't say, but where he is there's a lot of pain. If you let me, I can take that away."

She looked down at Eden. Sweat streaked his forehead as he thumped against the pillow and clacked his teeth together in rhythm. There was so little of him left, and the less of him there was the more desperately she clung to it. And now this, his pain or his insanity; whatever it was, it was something else she was being asked to let go of.

Mary stood over his bed as he thrashed and clacked his teeth. Then, slowly, a redness spread in his mouth. She looked into it for a moment as though something sensual were returning to that parched space, but as she saw what it was she winced and raised a hand to her own mouth. Gabe saw it too, and pinned my friend's head to the side so he wouldn't choke.

He'd bit off part of his tongue.

E den's mind wasn't gone. It was the clearest it'd been in years. Frantically he clacked, trying to give his message—END, END, END—and then, all at once, he felt Gabe's meaty paw leaning down on his neck, pinning him to the side. In the back of his throat was a warm iron taste. His senses were dull, but he knew he was breaking apart. Still, every part of him said: struggle. He needed to be heard and in that desperation he felt a freedom he hadn't known since the pressure plate, the freedom of a purpose. Dear God just let them know that I'm in here just let them know I want to end this let them know let them know please God.

He could smell Gabe on him, like a fog, his rank sweat. That big strong bastard, he thought, no one's going to shut me up. He kept clacking his teeth and thrusting against the arm that pinned him down. He wouldn't stop even if the only person who could feel his message was the same person who was trying to silence him.

He thought he smelled soap and water in the room. Was she also close and watching this? He could see the light from the lamp, but strained to see the shadow in the light which might be her. He needed her and thrashed his body some more, trying to look around, but still the arm pinned his head to the side. He could feel the calluses on Gabe's palm grinding against the charred skin of his face.

He grew too tired to buck, but still he clacked with his teeth. And as he lay there, he began to feel a wet warmth trickle down his cheek and pool by his mouth. He inhaled the wetness and it slurped past his forever-dry lips. It became difficult to breathe. Then the strong hands flipped his head to the other side, where a puddle hadn't yet formed. Still they pressed on him.

Now there was another shadow in the room, breaking up the light from the lamp, coming near him. It was her. It had to be.

The shadow wandered toward his bed, coming closer. It teased him like full clouds, yet to rain, wandering over cracked and droughty earth. He pushed against the arms that pinned him to the bed, blocking his view. He craned his neck, straining to see the dark rumor of her. He thought she would come to him, pet his head and give him what he needed: her, just to listen and to hear the very little he had left to say.

Through his bedsprings, he felt more movement in the room.

Another shadow mixed with hers. The other shadow came closer. He clacked his teeth harder and again bucked against his pillow, banging out the same message in tap code. It was useless,

Gabe's strong hands held him down. This other shadow mixed with what he thought was hers and soon he'd lost track of who was who. Then he watched one of the two leave the room, and he felt the vibrations of a door shutting. He felt suspense in that brief moment, the same as when a coin is tossed, caught in one hand and slapped on the back of the other, covered and awaiting the verdict of heads or tails.

The remaining shadow approached quickly and straightways, with a purpose. Then, on his side, against a soft and unburnt patch of skin, he felt the sucking coolness of alcohol. He bucked and gnashed his teeth and spit up the iron-tasting warmth that was liquid in his mouth.

She hadn't heard his message. She'd gone and signed the consent form.

The needle pricked and there was a biting warmth that spread into a hot blot inside him. Now the thick arms that had been holding him loosened. He tried to bang his message against his pillow, but something soft and even heavier than the man's arms pulled him down. It was the lamp across the room. He sunk into its light, which spread, unyielding, until everything became white and there were no shadows left and he was lost in all of it.

Before we deployed I lived in the barracks, and in the barracks, the privates and lance corporals bunked three and sometimes four to a room. No kitchen, just a head, four cinder-block walls, some beds and some footlockers. One of the privileges a corporal had was his own room. But it didn't seem like a privilege to me. I was lonely there. The ruts in the carpet where beds had been, the peeled paint where posters used to hang and the extra footlocker that had never been dragged out, these were all things that made me lonely. On the weekends, when the chow hall was closed, I ate lots of takeout, Chinese mostly, and having meals like this made me loneliest of all. So I bought a hot plate and sometimes cooked for myself. I'd fry a steak or make an egg on the one burner. It helped. Everything associated with preparing a meal helped: cleaning a dish in my bathroom sink, washing a pan, keeping utensils in my desk drawer and making trips to the PX for a few groceries.

That's where I bumped into Mary again.

It was a Saturday, just before Thanksgiving, and we still had a couple of months until deployment. It'd been weeks since that night in the gym parking lot and I hadn't been back to see her since. I'd walked to the PX from the barracks, and as soon as I grabbed a basket and turned down the first aisle, she turned down its opposite end with her shopping cart. Had I seen her sooner I probably would've avoided her, gotten my groceries elsewhere, or not at all, maybe just ordered Chinese again, but there she was, and I wondered if she would've avoided me given the chance.

Her shopping cart was nearly full and she pulled up alongside me and we talked. She told me that Eden was out of town training. She couldn't remember the course or if he'd even told her what it was. I told her it was a medical course and that I was going to the same one next week, missing out on Thanksgiving. She looked away when I said this, as if searching for something on the shelves. I think she was upset, though. Not that I was going, but that I knew what course he was at and that she didn't.

Then she looked at my basket. "Just picking up a few things?" she asked.

"Dinner," I said. "You?"

She looked at her full cart. "Dinner," she said.

A quiet moment passed between us, and in that moment it seemed one of us should move, but neither did. Finally she said: "You want company?"

I nodded and was glad for some company while I shopped. I took a packet of marinade from one of the shelves. My idea had been to panfry yet another steak.

"I've got plenty here for both of us," she said. Her cart was filled with simple ingredients: a couple of onions, some pasta and a little bread, nothing fancy, nothing like Eden would've made.

I had thought that the company she'd offered was for the shopping trip, but now I realized the invitation was to cook me dinner at her house. A thankful yet grim look passed between us like what passes between two people when one saves the other from stepping into oncoming traffic. But I wasn't sure which one of us was choosing to step into traffic.

We loaded groceries into the back of her car and barely spoke on the drive to her house. Eventually, I asked her something about work and she replied: "Fine." But I couldn't think of anything else to say. She turned on the radio and after one song we pulled into her driveway.

She put the car in park, but didn't get out. She switched off the music and looked straight through the windshield, as if into that place where her strength was. The car still idled and then she turned off the ignition. We were held in the silence between us. It made its own noise: a quiet like ringing. Then she looked hard into my eyes, as if reaffirming some decision she'd already made.

She got out of the car and went inside, leaving

115

the groceries and dinner in the trunk. Behind her, she left the front door open. I followed, stepping into the small entryway and glimpsing her heels as she walked quickly up the stairs. Most of the lights were on in the house and I could see the photos of her and Eden on the small table in the entry and also the photos of them hung along the stairs. In the hallway above, she moved quickly between the rooms. I could hear her scrambling as I walked up to the second floor. The house dimmed as she went from lamp to lamp, turning out each one.

Then it was completely dark.

I stood at the top of the stairs, by the banister. She found me there and grabbed my arm above the bicep, not my hand. She led me into a room. The moon was just rising and a little light came in from a glass sliding door that opened onto a porch. It was a pale light, and she looked silver and beautiful in it. She shut the blinds and again it was completely dark. As purposeful as she was, I knew she was fragile. This was their bedroom. I wanted this, but it was something I could ruin by the slightest miscalculation, so I sat on the edge of the bed like a child in a room of adults, moving very little, trying to behave.

She jointed her legs between mine and stood there for a moment. My head was at her breasts and the soft smell of her rested sleepily on me, slowing everything down. I reached my arms up her back and felt the rough lace of her bra beneath my fingers, but I didn't feel like I had permission to do anything more. She shifted in my arms, trying to lose her body's awkwardness by fitting into mine. I thought we might kiss, but instead she collapsed on me and I fell back onto the bed. She breathed near my ear and it felt like a stale wind. My hands were still on her back and she shook a little, like a branch pulled on too hard and then let go. And then she stopped and it was like that same branch had snapped. She couldn't go any further, so I rolled on top of her. She looked at me, touched my face and then crudely went for my pants, unfastening first mine and then hers. As we worked our hips free, I stopped and asked if she had anything for me.

"You don't need one," she said.

"I think I better."

"Really you don't," she replied and then looking away added: "I'm already pregnant."

Having come this far there was nothing to say, so I eased into her. And as I did, she looked back at me.

All through it, her eyes never left mine but her look was cold. She studied my face like it was an equation to be solved on a page. What we were doing wasn't a reckless and passionate infidelity, but a decision calculated by her. Then, when it was done, I started to move my hips off hers, feeling defeated. And it surprised me when she reached up and held me inside her. Still she didn't say anything and she wouldn't let go. Her face remained a mask of concentration. Her lips moved in little trembles. It was like she was counting.

To stop her lips, I kissed them and reluctantly she kissed me back.

She then rolled out from under me. We sat up on either edge of the bed and, facing away from each other, fixed our clothes. There was a lamp on the bed's end table. Once she was dressed she didn't turn it on. Instead she opened the curtains and everything in the room became dim and silver in a cold type of light.

"I wanted a child for a long time," she said, looking out the window. I wasn't certain who these words were meant for. Not knowing what to do, but wanting to be kind, I stood behind her and kissed the top of her shoulder. She spun around. In the look she gave me, I knew this had been the wrong thing to do. I stepped back and the space between us became cold as the light.

"I'm sorry to have brought you into this," she said.

"I'm sorry he's leaving," I said. "I didn't know about the baby."

"Neither does he."

I wanted to ask her why she hadn't told him. I wanted to tell her that if he knew about the baby, he might not come on this deployment. There was still time. They'd drawn up his reenlistment papers, but he hadn't signed them. He'd made nothing more binding than a promise at this point. But before I could tell her any of these things, she walked away from the window and turned on the lamp. Standing with her in their bedroom, after what we'd done, I had no right to try to help either of them. I'd stolen my moment and wanted to go back to the barracks, to be alone.

Not wanting to be any trouble, I asked her to order me a cab. By the time I got to my room it was late and I still hadn't eaten so I called the Chinese place, but it was closed.

After Mary signed the consent forms she sat outside Eden's hospital room, waiting. She could hear the muffled thumping of his head against the pillow and Gabe's inaudible voice, talking with one of the doctors as they delivered the sedative. They'd assured her this was powerful stuff and that it would dull his pain, making the end easier. They'd been perfectly nice about it, but curt. Long ago she'd begun to resent the stream of doctors and nurses. She'd spent the last three years dealing with them. They came and went and none had been in this ward, or at this hospital, as long as she, and all of them offered advice so freely on her husband's life and now on what they told her was his death.

Mary sat there, clutching the release form, examining it for the first time. It was an unintelligible hieroglyphic of drugs: lorazepam, propofol, ketamine, sodium thiopental. It all meant nothing to her and she ripped up the form into small pieces and threw them into the trash can down the hall.

She returned to her seat and now, from Eden's room, she could hear only silence. From her pocket, she took out her cellphone. It'd been a couple of days since she'd flown back to the hospital and she wanted to check in with her mother. She dialed, and the phone picked up after the first ring. But before her mother could speak, she did. Mary explained everything: his heart attack and stroke, the medications they were putting him on and how, if she wanted, he could painlessly be taken away.

Her mother said little but listened.

"The staff thinks it's best to speed things up," Mary said.

"It's been long enough, too long," her mother replied. "He would've wanted what's best for you and Andy."

"And what's best for us?"

"He never had to go on that deployment," her mother said, her words becoming sharp. "It's all gone on long enough."

The phone went quiet for a moment. "That's not how it was, Mom."

"He abandoned you," her mother said.

Mary didn't reply. She could feel the weight of her guilt, for what she'd done with me that night. Always she carried that guilt with her. In her mind there was an opposite truth. In her mind, she'd abandoned him that night with me, when she tried to trap him at home with the baby we conceived.

"I just want you back here," said her mother.

"I know you do."

There was little left to say so they said they

loved each other and hung up. Soon the door from her husband's room opened and Gabe stepped into the corridor. In the fluorescent light he seemed older, the shadows finding more of his face to hang themselves on. There was another chair next to Mary's; he flipped it around backward, straddled it and wrapped his forearms over its top.

"He's sleeping," said Gabe.

Mary nodded.

"He's not suffering anymore."

She nodded again.

"I don't know how long it will be," he said, "but I can make it quicker and I can make it so he doesn't suffer at all."

Gabe didn't say anything else, he just sat next to her, and that was what she needed. Down the hallway, the afternoon sun poured through a western window, blanching the already white floors and halls into the type of brightness that made everything disappear.

Then Gabe turned to her one last time. "You know this is going to end."

She said nothing to him.

My friend awoke into a dream.

He stood in some middle place that was all whiteness. I found him there and stood next to him. He pointed to his side, to the spot where Gabe had stuck him with the needle. His skin was clean and smooth, lucent as if it were subtly out of focus.

"Do you think she wants them to kill me?" he asked.

I didn't know, so in his dream I said nothing.

The two of us sat down, cross-legged, as if the whiteness were a field of grass we waited in. All this time I'd watched him, but I'd never seen him here. Then he asked if I thought he was going to die.

"I don't know."

Then he apologized for nothing in particular, he just said I'm sorry. I said the same and in the same way. It wasn't an apology to each other; it was an expression of regret, for how everything had turned out.

"What's it like where I'm going?" he asked.

He'd always been my friend so I lied to him again. "It's better," I said. But I didn't know. I've always been in this place of whiteness waiting for him like it was some act of repentance.

I hope this is repentance.

Still, there may be nothing past this, and I wanted to tell him that, but couldn't. Even being dead, I worried I'd say anything to console a desperate and dying man.

So there was nothing to say.

Eden broke the silence between us by cracking his knuckles, one after another, savoring the work as his thumb clamped down over each finger. In this place his body was whole again. He began to shake his hands and make loose fists, pushing them into the opposite palms, cracking the joints all at once. He shut his eyes and breathed. Then, without opening them, he said: "You know it's easiest on us."

"None of this is easy," I replied.

"No, but what she's gone through is worse than what you or I have. We may have burned and bled, but we were never asked to wait. She's waited, they all have. They're trapped by us and they wait."

"She wanted to trap you with a baby," I reminded him.

"But she never asked me to wait," he replied, and looked out into this place where nothing came or went except the whiteness. Then he looked at me again. "Can I go back to her now?" he asked.

"I think so."

"And where will you go?"

"I'll be here," I said.

On Tuesdays her first class was at six a.m. Those mornings she'd open the gym and change in the locker room. By the showers there was a full-length mirror. Standing naked and alone, she'd dress in front of it. Her arms and legs were muscled from her work at the gym and her dark hair hung against clean white skin, the kind of skin that would never hold a blemish or a tan. Appreciating her unappreciated body made her resent the way Eden had abandoned it. To Mary, her naked reflection seemed like a masterful painting left to hang on a shabby wall.

Her last time had been with me, and it'd been a couple of months more since their final try parked at the beach. Since then Eden hadn't touched her and she was running out of time. She could feel the acid in her stomach and could see the lost sleep in her face. Still, if she could coax Eden to bed with her just once more she'd be able to claim the child was his. He would stay then, she thought. That had been their agreement once, when I first met them. With a baby he'd stay. She felt sure of this and sure that she could build a whole world on the small chance that the child wasn't really mine.

But Eden wouldn't touch her and the truth of

how she'd used me grew inside her, coming on a schedule. Then, on one of those Tuesdays, she ran out of time.

That morning, she changed in the gym as she always did and taught her early class and another before lunch. That was all she was scheduled for. She'd planned to use the afternoon for an errand, a trip to a lawyer's office to sign on to Eden's power of attorney. The deployment was only three weeks away and she'd need the power of attorney—car payments, mortgage payments— she'd watch over his domestic life until he returned. But when another instructor called in sick, she was asked to cover an afternoon class. So she rushed out during lunch, handled the power of attorney and came back with just enough time to change into her sweaty clothes but not enough time to eat. As she led her class through their fourth round of split lunges, her sweat turned cold and the world closed in on her. When she passed out, she tumbled forward and on the way down knocked her head against a kettlebell, setting a gash that was tidy as half a penny pressed into the skin. Her students rushed over to her and she quickly bled enough to slicken the studio's buff wood floor. They pressed white sweat towels to her head, and she pushed back at their arms, trying to stand on her own. When she came to her feet, the little crowd stepped away from her and she stumbled toward a workout bench by the studio's door. She sat there for a time, leaning forward, her elbows propped on her knees and her head pressed to the towel. Some of the blood trickled over her wrist and down the soft inside part of her arm.

When the gym owner came in everyone cleared out from the room. He was an unathletic man and his paunch swayed like a cow's udder. He brought Mary a cup of water and then took her by the arm and out to his car. As they walked she protested in a wheezy and weak way, she didn't want to see a doctor. He took her anyhow. It was a twenty-minute drive to the naval hospital and all this time she asked him to just bring her home. He ignored her, and when he dropped her off at the emergency room entrance, she was still asking to go home.

Two paramedics helped her inside. Rows of plastic chairs and hushed conversations filled the emergency room. With her head tilted back and a towel still pressed against it, she split her attention, eavesdropping on the conversations around her and listening to the steady mutter of daytime talk shows from the televisions hung in each corner. One woman, who was very fat and likely diabetic, sat on a motor scooter next to her son, a lance corporal, who was lean, muscled and handsome in his camouflage uniform. The woman was missing a leg, and the leg she had poked from beneath her cotton pajamas, throbbing into calcification and covered with dry, flaky skin, which flecked gray as bark off a dying tree. Mary felt no sympathy for the old woman, if anything she felt the resentment which the woman's son likely couldn't feel. He'd sacrificed this day, along with who knew how many others, to preside over his mother's decay.

On the other side of the waiting room was another mother, a beautiful girl, even younger than Mary. She had two children, twins it looked like. The three of them slept against each other, their faces puffy and the lids of their closed eyes reddened and seeping. They didn't sleep well, but stirred, moment to moment. The emergency room seemed like a way station where they'd collapsed after finishing just one leg of an interminable journey.

Mary leaned forward and took the towel from her head. She thought perhaps the cut had stopped bleeding, but as she touched it with the tips of her fingers it seeped again. Desperately she wanted to leave this waiting room. It wasn't the sick people who upset her. It was the dependence. Yes, it troubled her to see the old and the young who couldn't fend for themselves, but more than that it troubled her to see those who'd been forced to give up their best days to tend to someone else's worst.

On the far side of the emergency room two broad automatic doors swung open. A middle-aged nurse in scrubs passed by the receptionist's desk. In an announcer's voice she read Mary's name from a clipboard and peered out over the rows of patients in the room. Mary stood, heading toward the automatic doors. She moved quickly, prodded forward by the shame she felt when her name was announced as if she were one of these many who couldn't help themselves.

Past the doors, Mary followed the nurse down the whitewashed corridors. She struggled to keep up, her head swimming with each step. Finally they reached a small examining room. Mary sat on a blue vinyl table in its center, the wax hygienic paper crumpling beneath her.

"A doctor will be by in a few minutes," said the nurse.

She shut the door tightly and the noise of it rang in Mary's ears. Mary closed her eyes softly and everything became louder. Her heart thumped in her chest. Her head throbbed. She lay on the examining table and curled up, waiting for the doctor. She struggled not to pass out again. She held the sides of the table so if she did, she wouldn't fall to the floor. Now, more than ever, she needed to protect herself.

Eventually the doctor came into the room. Mary pulled herself up slowly and heavily. She felt as if her head wore a crown of fog.

"No need to get up," said the doctor, a resident.

She read from Mary's chart on the door. "Fainting spell at work?"

Mary nodded, wondering what else was written on her chart.

"You eat today?" asked the doctor, who laid Mary down and now pressed around her stomach, working her way lower and lower.

"No, I haven't had much of an appetite."

"How far along are you? Ten, twelve weeks?"

The fog that had rested around Mary's head lifted. This doctor was the first to put words to what she'd done with me.

Quietly, Mary began to cry.

"You didn't know?" asked the doctor.

Mary looked away. "No, I knew."

The doctor finished her exam and walked across the room. She rested Mary's chart on a counter and began to write. Mary sat up and watched her.

The doctor turned from her work and spoke again: "Command notification is mandated when a dependent visits the emergency room. Your husband's already called over, asking after you. We're required to update him on your condition." Then she placed her hand on Mary's arm. "I'm sorry." The doctor stopped speaking for a moment, not sure how to go on.

Mary wiped her eyes and set her jaw. After a few moments she began to bite her nails.

The doctor finished writing. She walked over

and in her hands she carried a thin hooked needle. Gently, she parted Mary's hair, smoothing it down so she could see the gash, its shape a half-moon. The doctor dabbed the wound with an alcohol swab. Mary's eyes widened, her skin stung and then everything became cool and painless.

The doctor began with the sutures. "I know a place out in town," she said with a voice that was lost in her work. Her face was now very close to Mary's, furrows streaked the doctor's forehead and her eyes trembled, her concentration holding like an outstretched arm carrying a weight. What she said next, she said slowly, each word given with the same deliberation as the needlework: "The man who does it is quick and neat."

"Neat?"

"There won't be anything to remind you of it when it's over."

The doctor pulled tightly on the last suture.

Mary winced.

The doctor leaned back, examining her work as though she were reading a menu. Satisfied, she crossed the room and stood at a counter, where she filled out a prescription for an antibiotic. She handed over the prescription and with it another piece of paper. On it was an address, written not in a doctor's scratch but in clean block letters for Mary.

"They can fill that on your way out," said the doctor. Then she looked at the other piece of paper. "I hope you're able to do what's right for you."

Mary clutched the paper in her hand and looked at the address. She knew Piney Green Road. She'd driven past it a hundred times. It was a quiet street islanded by half-vacant strip malls. It was one of those streets that had an empty and untraveled sidewalk where the grass cracked up through the pavement. A place where she'd never had a reason to stop.

When Mary left the naval hospital, she took a cab to her car at the gym. Then she started her drive home. It was late afternoon. She had a voicemail from Eden. He was already there, waiting for her. She took a longer way back and drove by Piney Green Road, just as a detour, she told herself, just to find the address she'd been given. Then, on the way, she passed a Days Inn. The rooms were cheap. She wondered if women came there afterward to rest.

The clinic was in one of the strip malls, in a shop front that was unoccupied on either side. When she found it, the sun was getting low. It was still open, though. Three cars were parked out front. She wondered about the cars and parked her own across the street. She reclined her seat and waited, but she didn't know what for. Just up the block from her was the road sign. She loved the name—Piney Green—and the determined grass growing up through the pavement, trying to be in some part worthy of its namesake.

She waited until the sun had almost set. Then the door to the clinic opened. A girl, not much younger than she, walked toward one of the three parked cars. She had long red hair and was alone. She wore plain blue sweats and under her arm she carried a pair of jeans and a blouse, clothes from before, it seemed. She walked around the side of the strip mall and threw them in a Dumpster, then she climbed into her car. The girl sat there for a moment, seeming to make a call. Then she drove off in the direction of the Days Inn.

Mary pulled out from her space. She'd need to drive past the Days Inn to get home, but she didn't want to follow after the girl. Instead she took a back way. When she finally arrived, it was dark. Eden's car was in the drive and the lights were on in the house.

Eden could see nothing but the difference between light and dark. He could hear even less. Everything was very still, and his thoughts, clear. He knew exactly where he was. He thought this might be the last time he was ever awake and alone. He knew what Gabe was coming back to do. He knew when he next felt the cool alcohol swab on his side this would signal his end. He didn't feel afraid, or much of anything. It was just something he knew. How many times had he been shot at on deployment, or how many nights had he lain awake before a patrol wondering about dying and feeling afraid, even when death was a remote thing, and now, he knew a man would soon come with a needle to end him.

Strange, he thought, to feel so little about it.

If that's what Gabe was going to do, Eden wanted some say in it. He wanted that dignity. But the tap code hadn't worked. Despite the violence of Eden's attempts, no one had recognized it. And so it occurred to him to try something simpler. Something to show he was alive, nothing more. Slowly he clacked his teeth again: clack, clack, clack, clack, clack . . . clack, clack. Shave and a haircut . . . two bits. He kept it up, over and over. It was a jolly sort of clacking, not desperate as before. He sung it happily as if he were whistling his way through a park, or humming in the shower.

Then he felt a heavy shifting next to him. It was Gabe. He'd been sitting in the room this whole time. Eden struck his teeth together, clacking out the steady five-and-two rhythm, but he could feel his heart racing. The room was still dim. He could see nothing of Gabe in the light. But he could feel him. He was close, and then he leaned on Eden's bed and reached over him.

Eden could smell him now and he smelled clean, but in an unpleasant and fake way, like how a dog smells when it comes back from the groomers, clean but still a dog. Then Eden felt Gabe's heavy palm on his chest. His heart pumped deep and hard. Gabe must have felt it, too. Eden was waiting for the pinprick now, the last one. He did all he could. He kept up the clacking, beating his tune as he went under, like some idiot brass quintet on a sinking ship. He wanted to think about the simple rhythm, nothing else. Not Mary, Andy or me, not the day in the Hamrin and the smell of violence mixing with the smell of pines, not the years he'd spent in this bed, and most of all not about what was coming. He just wanted the clarity of that old five-and-two rhythm. Shave and a haircut . . . two bits.

Gabe's other hand moved onto him. But it wasn't the pinprick that came next. Gabe's fingers drummed something out: tap, tap, tap, tap, tap . . . tap, tap.

Eden stopped.

He'd been so ready for Gabe to take him away and now he didn't know what to do.

Gabe had been watching the whole time. He sat on the sofa, where Mary usually sat, holding the syringe, ready to go. This one injection wouldn't quite kill Eden, but it'd put him under for good, then, soon after and without pain, he'd fade away completely.

Gabe came to the bedside and the needle was primed, its tip wet. He took what he believed to be a last look at Eden, who'd begun clacking his teeth again. With that look, a thought came to Gabe, clear as an idea upon waking: it's shave and a haircut. Gabe drummed out the rhythm on Eden's chest, giving it a try. Eden became silent. Gabe set the syringe down. He had thought Eden's clacking was a tick from a failing brain, the synaptic electrocutions reading out along his clenched jaw. But to stop, this was a reaction to what Gabe had done—a reaction meant you were alive.

So Gabe kept tapping. He wanted to see if Eden would start again.

It was a test.

That night when she returned home from the naval hospital Eden had been cooking. The house was lousy with the smell of it. She came to the top of the stairs, where the kitchen and living room were connected and where the table had been set. He'd made salmon beurre blanc, a dish that was usually easy for him, but it hadn't come out well. On their plates it looked burnt. Eden sat at one end of the table. Roles reversed, he acted every bit the cliché of an angry wife waiting for a philandering husband.

The meal was a trap, though. That much was obvious to Mary. If he cooked she'd have to eat, and if she ate she'd have to answer his questions about all the things he'd now figured out.

They sat.

He served her.

Each waited for the other to speak.

She picked flecks of burnt skin off the salmon. As she ate, a mound of char slowly piled up on the side of her plate. Without the skin, the fish tasted fine. Hatefully, Eden watched her and shoveled down burnt mouthfuls, skin and all.

Finally he asked: "How far along is it?"

She told him and cleared his plate, bringing it over to the sink.

He said nothing, but soon realized it'd likely happened while he was gone at the medical course. "There's dessert in the fridge," he said. He'd made strawberry ice cream the week before. She served it into two glass bowls and sat one in front of each of them. Slowly they ate, their spoons clinking against the bowls.

"I wanted it with you," she said; her eyes hung in her bowl and her voice choked around the words. She took a bite of the ice cream and it felt good on her throat, the way it feels good when you're sick. She was crying now. "There's a place on Piney Green Road," she said.

"You don't do that when you're married," he snapped back.

He stood from the table and took their bowls to the sink. He washed them while she wiped her eyes with a napkin.

"I don't want it if it's not yours," she said.

She looked up at him, and as he cleaned he quietly told her: "I could never forgive you if you did that." She'd expected him to want rid of it, but he wouldn't abandon her child. And as she looked at him she felt it was his child more than anyone's, even more than hers. He would suffer the most for it.

Gabe sat by the edge of the bed. His palm rested on Eden's side, on that soft patch of skin where the needle would go. Gabe continued to tap: shave and a haircut. He watched for some reply. He wondered what was there, holding on. Gabe refused to quit: tap, tap, tap, tap, tap . . . tap, tap. Over the hours the rhythm began to tweak his wrist. In total he'd spent three days with Eden, and it was almost morning now. Gabe had barely slept and he felt the weight of his work in his eyes and clouded thoughts. Thin sheets of light entered the dark room. So too did morning noises, traffic, birdsong and softly heard voices. Then a familiar voice brought clarity. It was the clacking of Eden's teeth and the rhythm: 5, 1 / 3, 3 / 4, 1—END.

And Gabe was listening.

Mary called. She asked me to meet her at Onslow Beach in the afternoon. It was the Sunday before we deployed. The message she'd left on my phone hadn't said why, she'd just said that she was going to be there and that she needed me to come.

I hadn't seen her since that night at her house.

I got there early. I parked and then walked onto the beach through a split in the dunes. This was the deepest part of winter and I could feel the cold sand through my shoes. The air was very clear and in it seagulls floated on an offshore breeze. I sat on the sand. Some weeks before, a storm had come through, and down the beach a bulldozer was rebuilding the dunes.

Behind me, her car pulled up. I stayed sitting down. She came through the split in the dunes and looked past me, to the ocean. The waves lapped easily on the smooth, wet beach. It shone like a sharkskin. Then she saw me just behind her. She wore jeans, a baggy sweatshirt hid her stomach. Her dark hair was pulled back in a ponytail. The wind ran in her face, her eyes watered and it looked like she'd been crying. But I knew she hadn't.

I stood up. She sat down.

I sat down.

"You heard our news?" she asked.

"Let's talk in the car," I said. "It's freezing."

She ignored me. "It's not yours," she replied.

"Is that why you wanted to see me?"

"I didn't want you to wonder about whose it was." Her eyes wandered down the beach, toward the bulldozer. She began to shiver a little.

"You told me you were pregnant that night. I hadn't been wondering."

"Good," she said and didn't say anything else. We sat like this for a while. The seagulls overhead soon grew bored with us and floated farther out to sea. She kept her look fixed down the beach, away from me, toward the dunes that needed rebuilding. Turned like this, the offshore breeze was no longer in her face. Then she finally looked to me. Now her eyes were wet and red from crying, not from the wind. Quickly she kissed me on the mouth. Her lips were cold and slack. I would've returned her kiss, but she didn't give me the time. She stood and walked back through the split in the dunes. I heard her car start and she left. I sat on the beach for a long while. The sand became colder. The seagulls flew back inland and the driver on the bulldozer finished his shift.

The day we deployed Eden and Mary woke up together. The only light in the room was from the digital clock's red numbers on the bed stand. It was four a.m. She turned off the alarm before it could start and Eden turned on a lamp. He had to be at work by five and the buses would take everyone to the air station at six. He put on his uniform. She put on yoga pants and a T-shirt and her bump showed through the T-shirt.

While she was in the bathroom he made them both coffee—it was too early for breakfast. When he handed her the cup she refused it. He apologized, forgetting that she could no longer have coffee.

Then he made her some tea and went out into the cold, to the driveway. Here he turned on the old Mustang, heating it up for her too.

When he came back inside he brought her coat upstairs. He helped her put it on. He even zipped the front, paying extra care to her stomach. He wanted to be kind in the way a good father should be to a mother.

As they walked downstairs to the driveway, he gave her his one free hand and held both his coffee and her tea in the other. She didn't need his help with the stairs, it seemed like a silly gesture to her, but still she took it. His bags were already loaded in the back of the car, and as they got in she insisted on driving—that was for her to do. Despite how much she wanted him to stay, she'd be the one to drop him off.

During the ride in neither of them spoke and on the road there were few cars. They drove past the gym where Mary had worked—being pregnant, she'd since quit the job. At this hour its parking lot was empty. In a couple of hours, when she drove back, it would be filled with the cars of her old students. Then, a little farther down, they passed the Days Inn. Up ahead she could see the turnoff to Piney Green Road. The traffic light switched from green to yellow. She accelerated toward the intersection. The light went red and she ran it. She couldn't imagine sitting beneath that road sign with him.

Mary slowed the car down and Eden looked over at her. "Maybe when I come back we'll try to find a place closer to the beach," he said.

Mary glanced back at him. Traffic lights and neon signs shone against his face, reflecting too many colors at once. "With the baby it'd be nice to be near the beach," she said.

"We could take her for walks there."

"When do they learn to swim?" she asked.

"Three, I think."

"Three," she replied. "That's not so long to wait."

They parked a few blocks away from Eden's work. He wanted to say goodbye to her in private, without everybody else's goodbyes crowding in. She climbed out of the car and into the cold. He heaved his duffel bag and rucksack from the trunk. They stood by the front tire. The car's hazard lights flashed in the darkness. Far away from them the first of the morning etched out black treetops against a bluing sky. They looked at each other as though they might kiss, but they couldn't. Instead she held his hand on her stomach. "You want this," she said.

He nodded.

I won't give up on you again, she thought, and felt this promise like a tear in her heart.

Two days after he left, Mary made a trip back to her lawyer's office. She needed to pick up Eden's power of attorney. The lawyer gave her an envelope with it and some other paperwork inside. One of the papers was a copy of Eden's life insurance policy, Form Number SGLV 8286. Reading over the document, she saw the money hadn't been left to her. At first glance the name in the recipient box was one she didn't even recognize, but strangely the address listed beneath it was her own. Then, holding the form, she understood. The money had been left to her daughter and Eden had already picked the girl's name: Andromeda.

Mary dropped Andy at daycare and walked quickly over to the main hospital. When she came out of the elevator, Gabe was waiting for her on the fourth floor. Mary walked straight toward Eden's room, but Gabe stood in front of her. He asked her to sit with him in one of the chairs that lined the corridor. She looked past him, at the door to Eden's room.

Then she sat.

Gabe started by explaining Eden's stroke, and how sometimes a stroke can reawaken parts of the brain that might have been traumatized before. He told her how Eden's stroke on Christmas night might have brought some dormant parts of him back. As Gabe talked, he could see a crazy type of hope spreading through Mary. He knew she wondered what else might come back. These were dangerous optimisms and Gabe tried to diffuse them. He told her: "Waking up has put him in more pain than ever. It's not fair to keep him in this condition for long."

"Fair?" she said.

Gabe then explained how he'd figured out the tap code. He also explained that Eden would send only one message. Then Gabe told Mary what that message was and she looked away from him and rubbed the back of her neck. Gabe could see she was upset, but he went on: "It's what he wants. He won't feel any pain."

She looked back at Gabe. "Can I see my husband now?"

The two of them stood and walked down the corridor. Mary went into Eden's room alone. The lights were off and daylight seeped in from beneath the blinds. The steady and familiar sounds of his vitals pinged in the quiet. She climbed onto his bed and lay on her side next to him, careful not to disturb the tangle of wires that tethered his body to the machines. She placed her hand against his side, on the smooth patch of skin, to let him know that she was listening. He began to clack his teeth, just as Gabe had said he would.

END, END, END, he asked his wife.

Eden waited for what she would tell him. His mind was clear. With her near, he felt ready. He wondered when her palm would move away from his side. He'd feel the sticking of the needle there, and then the end. He didn't want to leave her. She'd given him everything, herself and a daughter when he couldn't have one. She was a fine wife, he thought, all she'd ever wanted was him.

Then he felt her message tapped out against his side: 3, 3 / 4, 3—NO.

He looked up at the dark shadow of her, disbelieving that she wouldn't give him this last thing. He tapped his message again and harder: END.

NO, she tapped back.

He thrashed in his bed. He felt her pin him down. He writhed against her, clacking his message. Why can't you find the strength to let me go, he thought. You gave up on me once, do it again, do it when I need you to. His mind twisted over itself, bending into dark corners. Still he tried to work at his message, but he began to lose the clarity of his intentions. Now his clacking receded into an unintelligible jaw grinding. His mind slipped into a rage. The parts of him that had been in focus began to melt, forming into some new amalgam. His mind lapsed, but his vision became clearer. His body continued to thrash, harder and harder, finding reserves of strength he didn't know. The door to his room opened. Everything filled with light. Now, being able to see again, Eden caught a full glimpse of Gabe rushing toward his bed. The big nurse looked older than Eden had imagined. He caught a glimpse of Mary too, and he could see her holding him down. She also looked older. And her face was all strength and conviction. For the briefest moment he felt content seeing these people who gathered around him in their desperation.

Then he looked away from them, toward the light in the door. It began to wash out the entire room, turning everything to white. And before that light blotted out all he'd ever known or seen, something crept into his room from the corridor. It was the cockroach from before. It'd been there all along, waiting for him.

Something in Eden split. His world turned to white. He would've sworn he was dead except he could still feel the stubborn beating of his heart.

Those days when Eden awoke happened years ago. I've been here every day since, in this between space that is empty and white, waiting for him, just like she does. We both wonder what will happen to us when he finally goes. Maybe I'll pass on to another place where there is no waiting and everything has ended. Maybe she'll go back to her mother and daughter, and her choices and memories will become far-off things. But those are distant worlds, and for now we remain here.

In the mornings she still walks into his room and takes her place on the sofa by his bed. Each day she places her hand against the smooth patch of skin on his side. On her good days she taps how her love for him remains. On her bad days she taps how sorry she is. Good or bad, though, he never reacts to these messages. But there is one thing he does react to. In the evenings, before she goes back to her room in the dormitory, she presses her hand against his side. Then she taps out what his number will be if he goes in the night. His reaction is subtle, but always the same: he shuts his eyes and he sleeps.

Sometimes, when he dreams, he and I meet in this between place. Always he's happy to see me and always we sit as old friends. We only ever talk about one thing, and it isn't the Hamrin Valley, his time with her at Onslow Beach or my time with her at his house, and it isn't the choices Mary has made. What we talk about is our daughter and that we may have pain but not that regret.

Som natural tears they drop'd, but
  wip'd them soon;
The World was all before them,
  where to choose.
Thir place of rest, and Providence
  thir guide:
They hand in hand with wandring
  steps and slow,
Through Eden took thir solitarie
  way.
    —John Milton, *Paradise Lost*

With thanks to:
*Lea Carpenter,*
*Ben Fountain,*
*PJ Mark,*
*Diana Miller,*
*Robin Desser*
and
*Sonny Mehta*

# A Note About the Author

Elliot Ackerman is the author of the novels *Dark at the Crossing*, which was a finalist for the National Book Award, and *Green on Blue*. His writings have appeared in *Esquire*, *The New Yorker*, *The Atlantic* and *The New York Times Magazine*, among other publications, and his stories have been included in *The Best American Short Stories*. He is both a former White House Fellow and a Marine, and served five tours of duty in Iraq and Afghanistan, where he received the Silver Star, the Bronze Star for Valor and the Purple Heart.

Books are produced in the United States using U.S.-based materials

Books are printed using a revolutionary new process called THINKtech™ that lowers energy usage by 70% and increases overall quality

Books are durable and flexible because of Smyth-sewing

Paper is sourced using environmentally responsible foresting methods and the paper is acid-free

**Center Point Large Print**
600 Brooks Road / PO Box 1
Thorndike, ME 04986-0001 USA

**(207) 568-3717**

**US & Canada:**
**1 800 929-9108**
www.centerpointlargeprint.com